Lurking arour  he
haunted

Mrs Porteous in her
line-dancing outfit

...and the freaky
fainting goat

Susan Gates says ...

How did I get the ideas for this story? From all over the place. My husband told me about a creepy museum he visited on a school trip. Among the other stuffed animals, it had a moth-eaten grizzly bear with a fat pink tongue poking out. One boy got told off for putting a fruit gum on it. I was surfing the Net (looking for something else) when I found a fainting goat website.

And General Custer's false teeth? I can't exactly remember, except that I was visiting the dentist a lot at the time!

Some other books by Susan Gates

ATTACK OF THE TENTACLED TERROR
KILLER MUSHROOMS ATE MY GRAN
REVENGE OF THE TOFFEE MONSTER

Susan Gates

Night of the Haunted Trousers

PUFFIN BOOKS

PUFFIN BOOKS

Penguin Books Ltd, 27 Wrights Lane, London W8 5TZ, England
Penguin Putnam Inc., 375 Hudson Street, New York, New York 10014, USA
Penguin Books Australia Ltd, Ringwood, Victoria, Australia
Penguin Books Canada Ltd, 10 Alcorn Avenue, Toronto, Ontario, Canada M4V 3B2
Penguin Books India (P) Ltd, 11 Community Centre, Panchsheel Park, New Delhi – 110 017, India
Penguin Books (NZ) Ltd, Cnr Rosedale and Airborne Roads, Albany, Auckland, New Zealand
Penguin Books (South Africa) (Pty) Ltd, 5 Watkins Street, Denver Ext 4, Johannesburg 2094, South Africa

On the World Wide Web at: www.penguin.com

Penguin Books Ltd, Registered Offices: Harmondsworth, Middlesex, England

First published 2001
1 3 5 7 9 10 8 6 4 2

Set in 14/19pt Baskerville

Made and printed in England by Clays Ltd, St Ives plc

British Library Cataloguing in Publication Data
A CIP catalogue record for this book is available from the British Library

ISBN 0–141–30826–5

Chapter One

I t had finally happened. They were closing down Nursery Rhyme Land.

Grandad still couldn't believe it. He seemed lost and bewildered. 'How could they do this?' he kept saying over and over again, shaking his head.

'It's not like we didn't *expect* it,' said Liam sternly.

He'd given up trying to comfort Grandad and now he was trying to make him face facts. It was getting a bit urgent. This was Thursday. And tomorrow, the doors of Nursery Rhyme Land would close for the last time. Then the bulldozers would move in and smash the place down.

'They've been trying to shut you down for years. You know what people think of this place.

You've only got to look in your Visitors' Book!'
Liam waved the greasy exercise book from
Woolworth's under Grandad's nose. 'Look at what
this guy's written, for instance: "I am shocked and
disgusted! It shouldn't be allowed in this day and
age!" And this woman's put, "How *could* you upset
little kiddies like this? My grandson was scared out
of his wits."'

'They don't understand the craftsmanship
that's involved –'

'They don't care about that, Grandad. They
think Nursery Rhyme Land is really gross! This
person's written, "It made me feel quite sick! I had
to rush outside for some fresh air."'

'You can't expect everyone to appreciate it,'
said Grandad stubbornly. 'There's bound to be
some oddballs around.'

Liam sighed. It wasn't the first time they'd had
this argument. And Liam knew he would never
win it. Nothing would persuade Grandad that
people in the seaside town hated Nursery Rhyme
Land. They would cheer when it closed down.
Especially parents and teachers. They'd

campaigned hard against it – they thought it had a *very harmful effect* on children.

He tried once again to force Grandad to make some decisions.

'Grandad! We've got to clear everything out of here by tomorrow. What are we going to do with all the displays? Where are we going to put The Three Little Kittens Who Lost Their Mittens?'

'Awwww.' Grandad's face softened. He smiled fondly. 'That's one of my favourites!'

'If you leave it here, APUP will smash it to pieces, or burn it or something!'

APUP were Nursery Rhyme Land's fiercest opponents. They hated Grandad like poison. They thought he was a villain, a nasty piece of work – some of them wanted to lock him up and throw away the key. They were the Association for the Prevention of Unkindness to Pussies. And they were very scary people. Liam glanced through a crack in the wooden shutters.

'They're still out there,' he said.

They were matching up and down outside

Nursery Rhyme Land, shouting and carrying big banners that said, 'CLOSE THIS VILE PLACE DOWN FOR EVER!' Behind them, the sea sloshed in grey waves on to the sand.

Nursery Rhyme Land was the oldest attraction on the sea front. It had been there for over a hundred years. It was in a seedy shack, crammed in between a hot-dog stand and a bouncy castle.

It looked just right for tiny tots. Day trippers brought their kids in droves. But they only ever brought them once. Nursery Rhyme Land gave children nightmares. It was a ghoulish and creepy place. Even adults, as they walked around it, felt a tingling down their spines.

Liam could understand their point of view. He felt it sometimes – the hairs prickling on the back of his neck. It *was* spooky in here. All these glass eyes watching you …

Nursery Rhyme Land was full of lovely cuddly animals. The kind of animals children loved – rabbits, mice, kitten, puppies. But they were all dead. And stuffed. And what made your skin crawl even more was that they were all dressed up in human clothes, like miniature people, acting out the nursery rhymes.

Liam had tried to explain it to Grandad: 'Times have changed. People don't like this sort of thing nowadays, Grandad.'

'Well, they should like it!' Grandad had bellowed. 'It's educational. It's part of our town's history!'

'They think it's cruel.'

'It's not cruel. Every single animal in Nursery Rhyme Land died of natural causes!'

Grandad sat on an upturned crate with his head in his hands. He looked a bit of a wreck. He hadn't even put his false teeth in today. The trouble was, it felt as if his whole world was falling apart. Nursery Rhyme Land had been his livelihood since he was a lad.

He wouldn't admit he was wrong. He thought everyone else was wrong.

'Just look at The Three Little Kittens Who Lost Their Mittens,' he told Liam. 'People say it's tacky and tasteless.' He shook his head wonderingly. 'What's up with folk nowadays?'

The Three Kittens, like the other displays, were in a glass case on a table. They were dressed in frilly Victorian frocks and bonnets. They had little black button-up boots. One kitten was tabby, one ginger, one white. They were standing at a tea table spread with tiny silver tea things – a teapot, cups, saucers. Their nursery rhyme was stuck to the front of their glass case.

Three Little Kittens lost their mittens and they
*   began to cry,*
'Mee-ow, mee-ow,
Now we can have no pie.'

They were supposed to be crying. Their little paws were wiping their cold, glassy eyes. But it was the *way* they looked at you, sort of reproachfully. As if to say, 'Why did you stuff me and put me in this case? Why did you dress me up in these stupid clothes?'

And there was another thing too. All the stuffed animals were so old and decrepit that bits kept falling off them. People didn't like it, seeing a glass eye, or a bunny's tail or paw at the bottom of a case. It made them feel even more queasy.

'I try to keep everything in good nick,' Grandad grumbled. And he did. He was always fiddling about, sewing midget frocks, repairing mini top hats, gluing teeny-weeny teapots. They were really fiddly jobs. But Grandad had endless patience.

'It's getting too much for me now,' he admitted to Liam. 'Especially Who Killed Cock Robin? Only today the beak fell off the owl. And I haven't had time to glue it back on yet.'

Who Killed Cock Robin? was their most impressive display. It was in a monster glass case on a long table that took up the whole of one wall. It showed Cock Robin's funeral procession with all the birds of the air attending.

> *Who killed Cock Robin?*
> *'I,' said the sparrow, 'with my bow and arrow.*
> *I killed Cock Robin.'*
>
> *Who saw him die?*

'I,' said the fly, 'with my little eye.
I saw him die.'

Who caught his blood?
'I,' said the fish, 'in my little dish.
I caught his blood.'

Who'll make his shroud?
'I,' said the beetle, 'with my thread and needle.
I'll make his shroud.'

Who'll dig his grave?
'I,' said the owl, 'with my little trowel.
I'll dig his grave.'

The rhyme itself was enough to give small kids the collywobbles. But the display itself was much, much worse. The case was cram-full of every kind of stuffed bird you could imagine – skylarks, wrens, swallows. And all of them were dressed up in black coats with black top hats.

You couldn't see Cock Robin. He was nailed up inside a tiny wooden coffin. But the sparrow was at the back. He was in handcuffs, guarded by a weasel on a bike, dressed up as a policeman.

'Tiny tots love Who Killed Cock Robin?' said Grandad.

No they don't, thought Liam, it gives them the creeps.

But he didn't say anything. Nursery Rhyme Land was Grandad's pride and joy. It was like grown-up men who are model train freaks. You just couldn't convince them that every kid wasn't as keen on trains as they were.

'I must mend that weasel's bike,' Grandad said, sucking his gums thoughtfully. 'That chain's come loose.'

'What's the point?' asked Liam desperately. 'APUP have got this building condemned. They said it was dangerous. You've got to move out. There's no choice.'

Grandad wasn't listening. 'Doesn't *anyone* care how you stuff a weasel nowadays?' he pondered. 'It's a lost art.'

'Snap out of it, Grandad,' pleaded Liam. 'It's

the end of the line for this place. Curtains! Time to call it a day! Even the Friends of the Weasel are after your blood. They've put your name and address on their web site. You should go into hiding!'

'I will not go into hiding!' roared Grandad. 'I have nothing to be ashamed of! I'll lie down under the bulldozers! I'll defend Nursery Rhyme Land until my very last breath! After all, son,' said Grandad, sweeping his arm round the gloomy little shack, 'all this is going to be yours one day. When I retire you'll be taking over! Can't think why your mum was never interested. But it's a man's job really, running Nursery Rhyme Land.'

Liam gulped nervously. He knew how proud Grandad was of Nursery Rhyme Land. He knew it was a family thing. After all, it had been started by his own Great Great Great Grandpa Clamp in 1862. But when he thought about spending his life, as Grandad had done, keeping stuffed kittens from falling apart and mending a weasel's bike, a terrible dreariness gripped him.

There was something so dusty, so musty and

fusty about Nursery Rhyme Land. Outside there could be dazzling sunshine. The waves could be blue and sparkling. But in here it was always dim – a sort of twilight world. Sometimes your legs itched. You longed to escape. Breathe fresh air, be with your mates, have a laugh. Liam felt a lot like that now.

'We can't let the light in,' Grandad was always warning. 'It'll fade their fur. Their lacy frocks will go yellow.'

Liam shivered. This place belonged in the nineteenth century. But Grandad wanted him, Liam, to take it into the twenty-first!

'I'll tell you what, son,' said Grandad brightly. 'You can't swing a cat in my flat. There's no room for all these glass cases. I don't intend giving up – I'm staying here tonight for a start. I'm going to put up one heck of a fight. But if they do pull this place down, you've got a big bedroom. How about you keeping them there, you know, just for a few weeks, until we can find a new place to set up?'

No way, thought Liam.

What if he woke up after midnight in his moonlit bedroom, surrounded by stuffed creatures watching him? He got the jitters just thinking about it.

But he couldn't tell Grandad that he didn't want Nursery Rhyme Land. He couldn't be that cruel. It would make Grandad's whole life seem like a waste of time. It would break his heart.

'Your Great Great Great Grandpa Clamp would turn in his grave,' Grandad thundered on, 'if he knew what that lot out there were up to. On his anniversary too. And not just any old anniversary. But an extra special one!'

Liam didn't need reminding. Grandad had been talking about it for weeks. It was one hundred years today since Grandpa Clamp died. Liam's grandad was always full of praise for Grandpa Clamp. He wouldn't hear a word said against him. 'That man was a genius!' he often said. 'I'd like to meet him and shake his hand! We owe all this to him. Without him, Nursery Rhyme Land wouldn't exist.'

Whenever he raved on like this Liam tried to

look grateful. He tried to be respectful
too. But he couldn't help thinking,
Grandpa Clamp had got a lot to answer for.

'They're still out there,' said Grandad, spying
through the shutters. 'Marching around and
yelling. Haven't they got homes to go to? That
Mrs Porteous, she's the worst of them. A really
tough cookie, that woman is –'

Mrs Porteous was the President of APUP. She
lived in a shell-covered bungalow, right next door
to Nursery Rhyme Land, and her mission in life
was to get Grandad's shack bulldozed off the face
of the earth.

'Some people say,' said Grandad in an awed
voice, 'that she was once a sergeant in the US
Marines. But that's just one of those daft stories,
isn't it?'

Liam wasn't so sure. Her vehicle, parked
outside her bungalow, certainly had a military
past. It was a Hummer jeep, as used by the US
Marines. Mrs Porteous drove it around town as if
she was going to war.

Liam sneaked a look outside. It felt as though

they were under siege. A large and fearsome lady was waving her arms about, giving orders. That was Mrs Porteous. Beside her, a girl was writing in a little black notebook.

What's she doing here? thought Liam.

He recognized that curly hair and those freckles. She was called Jessica. He didn't know her second name. She went to his school and was Chief Reporter on the school magazine. She once did a survey on school custard. She'd refused to write his comment (yellow dog-sick) down in her notebook. She hadn't even laughed.

Liam had thought at the time, Some people have *no* sense of humour!

Liam ducked down so she didn't see him. He kept quiet at school about his grandad owning Nursery Rhyme Land. Even his best mates didn't know about it. He wasn't one hundred per cent sure that they'd understand.

'That Mrs Porteous hates my guts,' said Grandad. 'And to think we were once childhood sweethearts. She gave me my very first kiss. She's a widow now, you know.'

'Yuk, Grandad!' Liam interrupted him. He didn't want to hear about Grandad's first kiss. The very thought made him squirm.

'Why don't they leave me in peace?' grumbled Grandad. 'Why don't they just clear off?'

But Liam knew that APUP would never clear off. Not until Nursery Rhyme Land was a heap of matchwood. They didn't trust Grandad. They were probably right – he was a stubborn old goat sometimes. They guessed he wouldn't go quietly.

'You shouldn't wind 'em up so much, Grandad,' said Liam. 'You deliberately drive 'em potty, don't you?'

'What, me?' said Grandad, looking innocent.

'I mean, what about those old trousers? What are you wearing them for? That's just asking for trouble! It's a good job APUP haven't seen them!'

'Don't care if they do,' said Grandad defiantly. 'It's a free country. I can wear what I like.'

'But they're made out of cat skins, Grandad!'

Grandad shrugged and said, 'They might be, they might not. Anyway, it's not as if *I* made 'em. These kegs are historical. They're probably over a hundred years old.'

Grandad had found the trousers when he was trying to sort out his stuff. They'd been in an old wooden chest that hadn't been opened for years. They were strange and wonderful trousers, a patchwork of furry pieces. Liam had never seen anything like them. But they certainly looked suspicious. Was that stripy patch a tabby cat? Was that a ginger tom? They were just the kind of trousers to send APUP into fits.

Liam sighed. 'Sometimes, Grandad, you're your own worst enemy –'

He could see the headline now: *CAT-HATER'S CRUEL TROUSERS OUTRAGE.*

'Why shouldn't I get up their noses a bit?' grumbled Grandad. 'They're trying to ruin me. I can't understand it. I've never hurt an animal in my life! I love animals!'

Liam sighed, more deeply this time. Not *this* old argument again. 'Look, Grandad,' he said, changing the subject, 'I've brought my digital camera.' It was hanging in a neat little black case from his shoulder. 'I'll take some photos, shall I? So you can remember Nursery Rhyme Land like it was?'

But Grandad wasn't listening. He still couldn't admit that APUP had won and he'd lost.

'And what about all me other bits and bobs,' Grandad was saying, 'that I've collected over the years? What about General Custer's false teeth?'

Grandad's other passion, apart from Nursery Rhyme Land, was the Wild West. When he was a young man he'd wanted to emigrate to America. Only Grandma (God rest her soul) had put her foot down. So he'd given up the idea and stayed in Nursery Rhyme Land instead.

Grandad walked past the Sing a Song of Sixpence display case, where twenty-four tatty blackbirds burst out of a plaster pie. He picked General Custer's false teeth up from their little stand. They were odd-looking gnashers, yellowy and joined together with big springs. If you clenched them too hard they sprang apart and hopped like a frog out of your hand.

'I didn't know General Custer had false

teeth,' said Liam.

'Everybody says that,' said Grandad, 'but that's because he kept it a secret. He was a really vain man. But after Custer's Last Stand, when he was killed along with all his soldiers, a Sioux warrior picked them up off the battlefield. Don't ask me how they found their way over to England. It's one of life's little mysteries.'

'Was General Custer one of your Wild West heroes, Grandad?' asked Liam kindly, trying to take Grandad's mind off the mess he was in.

'That rabid Indian-killer?' shouted Grandad. 'Hot ding! You must be joking!'

Liam had been listening to Grandad say 'Hot ding!' for years. Once he had asked him, 'Grandad, what does hot ding actually *mean*?' Grandad had looked flustered for a second. Then he'd said, 'It's cowboy talk, son. Like saying, "Goodness, gracious me," or "Well I never!"'

'No, I'm on the side of the Native Americans,' continued Grandad, giving General Custer's false teeth a quick polish. 'They weren't all warlike, no, not by any means. Some tribes were peace-loving peach growers. Even the warlike ones only raided cowboy camps to steal their frying pans –'

'Frying pans?' said Liam, completely baffled.

'Yep,' said Grandad. 'Those frying pans were made of extra-thin metal. Perfect for making arrows. In fact,' he said, marching off towards the back room with General Custer's false teeth in his hand, 'I think I've got some frying-pan arrows in one of the crates back here.'

But Grandad never got to find those frying pan arrows. Afterwards, Liam was never quite sure what happened. Nursery Rhyme Land seemed to grow even darker. But, in that darkness, he felt a kind of electric tingling, saw flashes of glassy eyes from weasels, birds and kittens. Heard a strange dry rustling and scrabbling …

What's going on? he thought, looking wildly around.

But then Grandad took all his attention. 'What are you doing, Grandad?' cried Liam, appalled.

Grandad was trying to cram General Custer's false teeth into his own mouth. With a suck and a snap they disappeared. Grandad clacked them experimentally together. They seemed like quite a good fit.

'No, Grandad, no,' said Liam. 'They're not your teeth. Take them out. You don't know where they've been!'

Too late. Grandad's face seemed to change, the muscles sliding around under the skin. It was still Grandad. But he had a different expression. A sort of cringing, beaten look. He scuttled suddenly into the corner and crouched there, shivering like a whipped dog.

'What's the matter?' begged Liam frantically. 'Speak to me, Grandad.'

Grandad opened his mouth. Big yellow rabbity teeth stuck out. A whining voice came through them. 'I'm sick bad, Master,' it sniffled. 'It's so awful cold. Don't send me out there again!'

It wasn't Grandad's voice. And it sure as shooting wasn't General Custer's.

Chapter Two

'Grandad,' said Liam, bewildered. 'Stop messing about. You're scaring me, Grandad. Why are you talking in that funny voice?'

But it was no use trying to contact Grandad. His body was there. But his mind didn't seem to be. Someone else had taken him over, sort of *borrowed* his body.

'I ain't yer grandad,' protested the stranger's voice.

Liam crept backwards, one step at a time. *Clink.* What was that? He leapt as if he'd been stung. He'd bumped into The Three Little Kittens case. The silver tea set rattled on the tiny table. The white kitten's ear fell off.

Liam shook himself savagely. Was he dreaming?

'Grandad, what's going on?'

'I told yer, are you a muddlewit or somefing? *I aint yer grandad!* I'm Rabbit. I'm Mr Clamp's apprentice.'

Liam's blood seemed to be roaring in his ears. He felt dizzy. He crept sideways, clinging on to the Sing a Song of Sixpence case to stop himself falling. Then he took a couple of deep, deep breaths.

'My Lor'!' said the voice, looking down at the cat-skin trousers. 'This is a turn-up and no mistake. Here I am wearing me own duds and wiv me very own teef in.'

Then Rabbit inspected his hands. 'Eh, wait a minute, I'm all wrinkles! Oh no, oh no. What's happened to me hands? I'm an old geezer. This ain't my body!' wailed the voice. 'Whose is it?'

'It's my grandad's,' said Liam in a dazed voice. 'What are you doing in it?'

'Don't ask me,' said Rabbit. 'I fort I was dead.'

Liam's brain spun out of control. It buzzed about wildly like a wasp in a jar.

He clutched at his head. 'I'm going crazy!' He

staggered and, as he did, he crashed into Rabbit. Rabbit made a grab for him.

'Watch it! Mind my –'

But Rabbit never got the chance to finish his warning. Liam, frantic to escape, jabbed his elbow into Grandad's ribs. Rabbit gasped, 'Oi!' and doubled up. His springy false teeth shot out and skittered across the floor. They came to rest under the Hickory Dickory Dock case.

Liam's eyes followed them. Then he turned his horrified gaze back to Grandad/Rabbit. The pink gummy mouth opened. Whose voice was going to come out?

But Liam already knew the answer to that question. For the face was changing again. The muscles wriggling like worms under the skin. The spine got stiffer, more defiant. Two stubborn eyes glared out at Liam.

'Grandad!' cried Liam thankfully. 'You're back! Are you all right?'

'What are you talking about?' said Grandad, jiggling his shoulders as if he was settling himself

23

back into his skin. 'I haven't been anywhere. Mind you,' he added, putting a hand to his forehead, 'I do feel a bit flushed, a bit giddy.'

He glanced down at his cat-skin trousers. 'I think it might be these trousers. They're too constricting for this warm weather. I'll just go out the back, put my grey slacks on again.'

Liam said nothing. He couldn't; he was too stunned. He looked helplessly round Nursery Rhyme Land. 'What's going on?' his brain begged him.

Twenty-four pairs of cold eyes goggled back at him from Sing a Song of Sixpence. But they didn't give him any answers.

'What are General Custer's false teeth doing under here?' asked Grandad. He'd got his grey slacks on now. The other trousers were hanging over his arm. He bent down to pick the teeth up. Absent-mindedly, he wiped the dust off them and put them in the pocket of the cat-skin trousers.

Liam watched, fascinated, as Grandad folded the trousers up and put them on the crate. He'd half-expected the teeth to take a froggy leap into

Grandad's mouth, right in front of his eyes, and Rabbit's voice to come whining out, 'Hello. It's me again.' But they didn't.

Suddenly, a startling fact rose to the top of Liam's bubbling brain. 'Those aren't General Custer's false teeth, are they, Grandad?' said Liam. 'They can't be.'

To Liam's surprise Grandad admitted it straight away. He sounded absolutely shameless about it. 'Of course they aren't,' he said cheerily. 'Between you and me, son, I made that all up. A little something extra to bring the punters in. It's the showman in me!'

'So whose are they?' asked Liam. He still felt shell-shocked. But his brain was beginning, feebly, to flutter back to life.

'Could be anybody's,' said Grandad, shrugging. 'Last time I looked in that old wooden chest, that's when I found 'em, oh, years ago. They're antiques, like those trousers. No knowing who they belonged to.'

Liam thought shakily, *I* know, although he wished he didn't.

And all the time the sensible side of him was trying to deny it: Get a grip! You didn't really see what you saw!

Maybe you had a brainstorm, he told himself. Maybe you got sunstroke. But how could you get sunstroke in Nursery Rhyme Land, where the sun never shone and where time had no meaning?

'Oh no!' said Liam, checking his watch. 'I'm supposed to be meeting Mum at the lab! I'm late.'

He was pleased to be in a rush. It meant he couldn't think about what had just happened. He snatched his skateboard from against the wall. 'Catch you later, Grandad!'

'I won't be hard to find,' said Grandad. 'I'm not moving from here. I'm not giving up. Like I said, I'm staying here tonight. I don't trust that APUP lot. If I leave this place empty they'll be in here like rats up a drainpipe.'

Liam shook his head sadly. Poor old Grandad – still fighting on though he'd already lost the war.

'I saw that Mrs Porteous at the dentist's not so long ago,' Grandad was rambling on. 'She was having her false teeth fitted, same as me. And I thought, hot ding! Romance could have  blossomed between me and that woman.'

'Get real, Grandad,' interrupted Liam, exasperated. 'She hates your guts! You said so yourself. She's the one that got this place condemned.'

But Grandad only sighed wistfully as if he was thinking of things that might have been. 'She's like a battleship with all guns blazing,' he said dreamily. 'I like a woman with spirit.'

Then Grandad seemed to recall something else. 'I nearly forgot! There's a young lass coming round from the local paper. Wants to interview me about Nursery Rhyme Land. She sounded nice over the phone. She says she's a real fan.'

'A fan?' Liam paused at the door, puzzled. He didn't know Nursery Rhyme Land had any fans.

'Be good publicity,' said Grandad.

Too late, thought Liam. Way, way too late. By the time an article appeared in the local paper, Nursery Rhyme Land would be rubble.

But he didn't tell Grandad that. He didn't have

the heart. Besides, it couldn't do any harm. Suddenly, Liam had to ask; he couldn't help himself. 'By the way, Grandad, did Great Great Great Grandpa Clamp have an apprentice called Rabbit?'

'How did you know that?' said Grandad. 'That's a very sad story …'

I don't want to hear this! thought Liam frantically. He could have kicked himself for asking.

'In a rush. Gotta go! Bye!' he told Grandad. Then he suddenly remembered his digital camera. He ripped it off his shoulder. 'Look after this for me, Grandad. I'm skateboarding to meet Mum. I'd hate it to get smashed.' Then he was gone.

He went scooting round the corner. APUP were still waving their banners. 'MR CLAMP IS A CAT-HATER,' one said. But Mrs Porteous wasn't with them. She must be taking a break from all that shouting. Jessica seemed to have gone home too. The others didn't look at him twice. The future owner of Nursery Rhyme Land was

sailing past them. But, luckily for Liam,
they didn't know that. To them, he was
just a scruffy kid on a skateboard.

Back inside Nursery Rhyme Land, Grandad
had put Liam's camera in a safe place. Now he
was combing three long hairs over his bald spot,
smartening himself up for the interview.

Then he heard something. From behind him
came a sound: *Tinkle, tinkle.* It was only a tiny
sound. You could barely hear it. But the muscles
in Grandad's back tensed up, stiff as an ironing
board. He knew what it was. It was the bell on the
weasel's bike.

Oh no! thought Grandad. It's starting already!

Every 7 April , every anniversary night, it was
the same. Weird things happened in Nursery
Rhyme Land. There were disturbances, strange
goings-on. Just tiny things, nothing to get really
alarmed about. That's what Grandad told himself
anyway. For instance, last year, when he'd come to
open up on 8 April, he'd found The Three Little
Kittens Who Lost Their Mittens had swapped
places inside their glass case. The white one

always sat next to the teapot. Now the tabby one sat there instead.

Grandad had tried to convince himself: 'Your memory's going. They always sat that way round.' But in his heart, he knew that they didn't.

Liam didn't know about any of this. Grandad hadn't told him. Grandad hadn't told him either that he had never spent a night in Nursery Rhyme Land. Especially not an anniversary night. This would be his very first time.

So, all in all, Grandad was feeling a bit twitchy. Plus, this was an extra-big anniversary, a hundred years. What if that meant extra-big 'disturbances'?

'Don't be an old fool,' Grandad told himself, relaxing a little. There were no bells now. His ears must have been playing tricks.

Tinkle, tinkle.

He whipped round, stared at Who Killed Cock Robin?, rushed up to the case and peered inside.

Constable Weasel stared back at him with blank, glassy eyes. His little paws were still stuck to the handlebars. They couldn't move if they tried.

'Old fool,' Grandad scolded himself again.

But there was a niggling question at the back of his mind. A question he'd asked himself hundreds of times before. Shouldn't he tell Liam there was something not quite right about Nursery Rhyme Land? Something, well, a bit sinister? After all, if he was going to inherit it, he really ought to know.

But like all the other times, Grandad decided no. No need to worry the lad. He loves Nursery Rhyme Land. It's his big ambition to take over when I retire. I don't want to put him off.

Grandad definitely didn't want that. He needed Liam, in a few years' time, when he was old enough, to take Nursery Rhyme Land off his hands. Grandad couldn't admit it, even to himself – but he was looking forward to retiring from Nursery Rhyme Land. He didn't want the responsibility any more. Handing it over would be a big relief.

He squinted in at the weasel.

'I was going to fix that bike,' he reminded himself uneasily.

But that would involve taking the back off the

glass case, reaching in and getting the bike and the weasel out. The weasel's fur was moth-eaten. But his tiny teeth sparkled, razor sharp.

'Think I'll fix it tomorrow,' Grandad decided.

Chapter Three

It tends to prey on your mind when your Grandad's body's been borrowed, even if it is only briefly, by a boy from the nineteenth century. On his way to meet Mum, Liam's brain was hopping with thoughts of Rabbit. He nearly skateboarded into several pedestrians.

He walked through the office door with Mum's name on it, Dr Janet Cooper, and Rabbit got pushed to the back of his mind, because Liam found himself right in the middle of a crisis.

Mum was in there with Milton, her wild-haired research assistant. She was waving a newspaper about.

'How did this happen?' she raged at Milton. 'How did all this information leak out? It's terrible publicity. Terrible!'

Mum was a scientist at the university. Her speciality was genetics. And today had been the worst day of her career.

'We might as well kiss goodbye to any more research money,' she fumed, throwing the paper on to her desk. 'It's a disaster! That goat is a dead duck!'

She went rushing out of the office. 'Oh hi, Liam,' she said as she dashed past him. 'Wait here. Be back in two ticks.'

She went striding out with her white coat flapping.

Liam stared open-mouthed after her. His mum was usually a cool customer. Nothing fazed her. He wasn't used to seeing her in such a state.

He propped his skateboard carefully against the wall. 'What's up?' he asked Milton.

'Cat's out of the bag,' said Milton mysteriously, 'and amongst the pigeons.'

'I thought Mum said something about a *goat*.'

'Yeah, well, it is a goat actually,' admitted Milton.

Milton rolled up the newspaper and stuffed it into the pocket of his lab coat.

'Show you if you like,' he told Liam. 'It's not a secret any more. We'll probably be on the six o'clock news on telly tonight.'

Liam liked Milton. He was a bit mad. But he was a sparky sort of person, always fizzing with fresh ideas. He cheered you up. You couldn't help catching his enthusiasm. But today even Milton looked downcast. Something really serious must have happened.

'OK then, show me,' said Liam. Milton went bounding off down the corridor, a skinny, springy figure in his hi-top trainers.

Liam lounged after him. Like his mum, he liked to look cool at all times. He never hurried unless it was for a special reason such as, for instance, trying to blot Rabbit out of his mind.

Oh no, I've just thought about Rabbit *again*! thought Liam. He gritted his teeth. Stop thinking about him! he ordered his brain. But as he pushed through a fire exit door after Milton, Rabbit's whining voice came back to him, clear as day. 'It's so awful cold. Don't send me out there again.'

'Shut up, shut up, shut up,' gabbled Liam, trying to put the lid on his boiling brain.

'What did you say?' asked Milton.

'Nothing.'

'I've got to warn you, you have to be quiet out here.'

'Why?'

But Milton just put his finger to his lips. 'Shush.'

He led Liam across to a small, grassy pen. The pen had a goat inside it.

It was a very pretty goat, small and pure white, skipping about, grazing peacefully on the grass.

Liam stared at it. '*Awwww*, how cute,' escaped from his mouth.

He was surprised to see it there. But it looked perfectly harmless. How had one tiny goat got everyone running around like headless chickens?

'Shhhh,' said Milton. He was tiptoeing up to the goat as if he was scared it might explode.

'Stay back,' he hissed at Liam. 'Your boots are too clumpy.'

'Eh?' Liam hissed back, bemused.

'This goat is at the cutting edge of modern science,' whispered Milton. 'It's a clone from a goat cell sent over by our research colleagues in America.'

'Wow,' Liam whispered back, impressed. 'A clone – like Dolly the sheep. What's its name?'

'Well, her official name is Cell Batch 1,203. But I call her Snowdrop.'

'*Awww!*' said Liam again. He was nuts about animals. It was a real treat to see an animal that was alive and warm and breathing. That was behaving like an animal should. Not dead and stuffed and having a tea party, like the creatures in Nursery Rhyme Land.

Then Milton put him right. 'Only, she's not behaving like a proper goat should.'

'She looks like a perfectly good goat to me,' protested Liam.

'She's got a major defect,' explained Milton. 'It shouldn't be there. But cloning is still very experimental.'

'What went wrong?' asked Liam.

'Watch this.'

Milton looked around him to check there was no one watching. He took the rolled-up newspaper out of his pocket. Put it to his lips like a trumpet. Puffed up his cheeks. Then blew an enormous raspberry note.

'*PARP!*'

Snowdrop dropped like a brick. She tumbled on to her back. Her four neat little hooves stuck up into the air. Her whole body went rigid, as if she'd been instantly frozen.

Milton calmly consulted his watch. He began counting, 'One, two, three –'

Liam was distraught. 'She's dead! She's dead!' he cried. Out of nowhere, another little voice tried slithering into his mind. 'I fort I was dead!' it said, surprised.

Liam ignored it. His whole attention was taken up by Snowdrop, who was still stiff as a plank. His fists flew to his mouth in great distress. 'You *killed* her!' he accused Milton. 'You killed her!'

'Nine, ten,' Milton concluded.

Miraculously, Snowdrop shivered. Her stiff limbs jerked to life. She scrambled to her feet.

Then, as if nothing had happened, she began peacefully chewing the grass.

'She passed out,' explained Milton. 'She does it all the time. When anything startles her, *whump*, she's out cold. Then in ten seconds she's right as rain again.' He shook his head. 'It's really abnormal. It shouldn't be happening. We've made a mistake. We've bred some kind of freak.'

'A freak!' Liam said angrily. 'She's not a freak!'

'That's what the newspaper calls her,' said Milton. 'Just look at this headline.' He unrolled the paper.

FREAKY FAINTING GOAT FIASCO AT FRANKENSTEIN LAB, it said. *By your roving reporter, Jessica Porteous.*

'She's made Snowdrop into a genetic horror story,' said Milton. 'It's really sensational stuff.'

Connections were being made inside Liam's head. Oh no, he was thinking, oh no.

'It's a shame,' Milton said, not noticing Liam's silence, 'because Snowdrop's a medical marvel. She's got drugs in her milk, insulin to help diabetics. She should be *good* news for people.

Now there's nothing but *bad* news about her. This article is way over the top. It says, "This lab should be shut down! They have cloned a monster!"'

Jessica Porteous, Liam was thinking. Naaa, it can't be her, writing stuff for a *proper* paper. How did she get to be such a hotshot reporter? The last I heard she was doing surveys on school custard.

'And the worst thing is,' said Milton, 'that all this is our fault. This cute little girl came round, all curls and freckles, and said, "I'm writing a piece for the school magazine." And somehow she got to see Snowdrop. Then a low-flying jet came over –'

'I get the picture,' said Liam. 'Snowdrop passed out. Jessica got a big scoop. And I think she's just about to get another one.'

'What are you talking about?' asked Milton.

'She's back at Nursery Rhyme Land interviewing Grandad,' said Liam. 'It's got to be her. And I bet you anything she's related to Mrs Porteous – that's Grandad's worst enemy!'

'Oh dear,' said Milton, who knew Grandad wasn't the world's most tactful person. 'You'd better get back there before he says something he shouldn't.'

'You mean something *else* he shouldn't,' said Liam bitterly. 'He's already up to his neck in trouble.'

'Well, this Jessica could sink him altogether. Don't underestimate her. She's dangerous. She's a wolf in sheep's clothing –'

'I gotta get back to Nursery Rhyme Land!' yelled Liam in a frenzy. 'Right now!'

Whump! He spun round. The startled Snowdrop had dropped as if she'd been shot. His loud voice had brought on another fainting fit. Her twiggy legs stuck out sideways this time. Her eyes were tight shut.

'Sorry, sorry,' said Liam. 'I forgot –'

'Don't blame yourself,' said Milton. 'Anything brings it on. A door slamming, a car back-firing, a crow squawking. We've cloned a goat that's a nervous wreck.'

'I know the feeling,' said Liam. He felt like a nervous wreck too. Especially when he thought about what might be happening back at Nursery Rhyme Land.

Maybe Grandad will keep his mouth shut, he thought desperately. But experience told him: 'Fat chance!' Then another, more terrible thought, sprang into his brain. What if he puts the cat-skin trousers on and the teeth in and Rabbit's voice comes out of his mouth?

That would be a scoop and a half for Jessica. That would be the biggest scoop of all time.

'Nine, ten,' counted Milton, as Snowdrop whisked her tail, jumped up and frisked round the pen. 'She's like clockwork, ten seconds and she completely recovers. It's all very strange –'

'What I don't understand,' wailed Liam, 'is how this Jessica could get articles in a newspaper. She's just a kid like me!'

'I can tell you that,' said Milton, shrugging. 'That's easy.' He flicked to an inside page of the newspaper. *Editor: Peter Porteous*, it said.

'Oh no,' said Liam, bewildered. He was beginning to think that, like Grandad, he'd been too long in Nursery Rhyme Land. 'I didn't know about any of this! These Porteouses are like the Mafia. Do you think that bloke's her dad?' he asked Milton. 'And that Mrs Porteous is her granny or something?'

'Wouldn't surprise me a bit.'

Grandad's done for, thought Liam. She'll stitch him up good and proper.

Grandad had hoped against hope that there was some chance left for Nursery Rhyme Land.

What's up with him? Doesn't he know when he's beaten? thought Liam grimly.

But he still had to get back. Everyone seemed out to get Grandad. They thought he was worse than Jack the Ripper! But Liam knew better. Liam was on Grandad's side, no matter what.

'Catch you later,' he whispered to Milton. 'Gotta go.'

The door crashed shut behind him, so he didn't hear the distant thud as Snowdrop went down for the third time.

He snatched a few words with Mum in her office. 'I'm staying with Grandad tonight,' he said.

'OK,' said Mum, shrugging. Liam often stayed the night with Grandad. But Liam's mum hardly ever saw her father. They had a very uneasy relationship. Mum wasn't interested in Nursery Rhyme Land. And Grandad wasn't interested in her research. They didn't have much to say to each other. They lived in different worlds.

But Mum still wanted to know if Grandad was OK. 'How's it going,' she asked, 'down in Nursery Rhyme Land? Is the stubborn old beggar going to go quietly tomorrow?'

'You must be joking,' said Liam. 'They'll have to carry him out of there kicking and screaming. He says he's going to lie down in front of the bulldozers.'

Mum sighed, then rubbed her forehead wearily. 'Typical,' she said. 'That's all I need. More problems. What with your dad being away and the press getting hold of this goat story –'

Liam was in a rush, but he needed to ask Mum a question. He hummed and hawed a bit – it was a very tricky topic. 'Mum,' he said, 'do you remember General Custer's false choppers?'

For a few seconds Mum looked baffled. Then her face lit up. 'Oh, those disgusting old things,' she said. 'They were your grandad's pride and joy.

You know he's bonkers about anything to do with the Wild West.'

'Did he,' asked Liam, wincing a little, 'did he ever, you know, *wear* those false gnashers instead of his own? And, and, did anything *weird* ever happen, you know, when he did? I'm not talking about General Custer's voice coming out of his mouth,' said Liam, as though Mum should be relieved to hear it, 'but someone else's. Like, for instance, this creepy Victorian apprentice called Rabbit?'

Liam's mum frowned. She looked at Liam as if he'd gone completely off his rocker. She started to say, 'Look, I know Grandad's a bit eccentric but –'

Then the phone rang urgently, *Brrrr, brrr.*

'Oh no,' said Mum, scrambling to answer it. 'That's probably the six o'clock news again, asking me for an interview. I'll be lucky if I've still got a job tomorrow. I'd like to wring that Jessica Porteous's neck.'

So would I, thought Liam. Has she got any idea of the damage she's done?

Then he remembered that she was probably doing more damage right at this moment, back at Nursery Rhyme Land. He grabbed his skateboard and took a short cut through the labs. He knew he wasn't supposed to be in there. Children weren't allowed. But that shiny floor made   the skateboard fly.

'Hey, dude,' warned Milton. 'Slow down!'

'In a hurry,' gabbled Liam.

He was going to scoot on. Then he did a double take. Milton had something spread out on the laboratory bench. They were teeth, about half a dozen human teeth.

For a moment Liam thought, I'm going mad. Yesterday he hadn't even *thought* about teeth. Today he was seeing them everywhere!

Despite himself, Liam had to ask, 'What are those for?'

'I collect famous teeth,' said Milton. 'I've got one of Queen Victoria's.'

Oh no, thought Liam, I *am* going mad –

Milton saw his appalled expression. He

hastened to explain. 'It's just a little
fantasy of mine,' he said, his eyes
sparkling with enthusiasm. 'We scientists are only
human,' he added. 'We have dreams too. Just like
everyone else.'

That didn't explain anything. But Liam was too
scared to ask more questions. He might find out
something he *really* didn't want to know.

His head was starting to ache. Why was he
wasting time listening to Milton? He had places to
go, things to do. He whizzed away, leaving Milton
burbling on in the background, and shot through
the fire exit.

'Oh, *no*!'

There was a muffled thud. Four little hooves
pointed skywards.

'Sorry, Snowdrop,' said Liam, wincing as he
zoomed off down the path. 'Sorry!'

Chapter Four

Liam was far too late to warn Grandad. Jessica Porteous already had her scoop. Or would have, as soon as the trousers she'd stolen were forensically examined by experts.

At five o'clock, when Liam was finding out about the fainting goat fiasco, Jessica had got Grandad wrapped round her little finger.

She had promised her gran, Mrs Porteous, president of APUP, that she would dig up some dirt, which would sink Nursery Rhyme Land for ever. And her dad, Peter Porteous, editor of the *Evening Chronicle*, was eagerly awaiting her next scoop. As she sat smiling sweetly at Grandad, Jessica was already making up headlines: *SHOCKING SCANDAL OF THE TROUSERS OF SHAME!*

Grandad approved of polite children. He thought modern kids (including Liam) had no manners. Which was strange because Grandad was hardly well known for his good manners. In fact, he was famous for being downright rude.

But Jessica charmed him from the first moment. Her Miss Goody-Two-Shoes act had him completely fooled.

'Excuse me, Mr Clamp,' she said. 'I've been meaning to do this for ages – I must write something in your visitors' book.'

She scribbled away. Grandad couldn't help peeking. When he saw what she'd written he glowed with pride. After pages of rude comments, at last someone had got it right.

'Nursery Rhyme Land is my most favourite place,' wrote Jessica. 'It is an inspiration to all us children!'

As if to prove this, she walked over to The Three Little Kittens Who Lost Their Mittens. She stared in. The kittens stared back. She tapped the glass. The white kitten's other ear fell off and dropped like a shrivelled leaf to the bottom of the case.

'How sweet,' trilled Jessica.

'Tut, tut,' said Grandad fussily. 'I must glue that back on. I like to keep everything shipshape. There's a lot of work in this place, believe me. People nowadays just don't appreciate the craftsmanship –'

He was on to his favourite topic. While he was telling her about fixing weasels' bikes and sewing frills on frocks, Jessica's sharp little eyes inspected the case even more closely.

Wait a minute, she thought. That white kitten's eyes just moved.

She *thought* they had flicked sideways to the ginger kitten. Just a quick glance. As if they were communicating with each other.

For a second she came over all hot and dizzy. She shook her head and looked again. All the kittens gazed straight ahead with a goggly-eyed, glassy stare. She must be imagining things.

Jessica scolded herself severely: Concentrate,

Jessica. You're here to do a job.

Since the *FAINTING GOAT FIASCO* she had got the taste for scoops. It was a big thrill – sniffing out scandals. Like turning over stones to see if there were snakes underneath.

Grandad concluded: 'And of course, you mustn't forget to take their eyes out and polish 'em so they look really lifelike. Are you getting all this down?' he asked her. 'I think your readers will be really interested.'

Jessica pretended to be busily writing in her notebook. But all the time she was checking the place out, looking for something incriminating. Something she could use against Grandad.

She didn't feel *very* guilty about it. No one liked Mr Clamp anyway. He had loads of enemies. APUP were out to get him. And the Friends of the Weasel were after his blood. You'd think, the way people talked about him, he'd have horns growing out of his head.

But, to her own surprise, she was finding it hard to hate him as much as she ought to. If he was that bad, why was he spending all this time talking to her? Patiently explaining things, not rushing her out of the door? Her own dad never had time to explain. You practically had to make an appointment to see him. And when you did, he always had one eye on his watch.

She was just thinking, And another thing, Mr Clamp doesn't talk down to you, just cos you're a kid, when she spotted the trousers.

Instantly, her reporter's nose twitched like a bloodhound's. She completely forgot about Grandad's good points.

'Excuse me, Mr Clamp,' she trilled, 'but what are those clown's trousers doing here?'

'Clown's trousers?' said Grandad, mystified. Then he saw where she was pointing.

'Oh those,' said Grandad. 'I wear those. I wear them all the time.'

He leaped towards them. He was eager to tell her about his cat-skin kegs. At last he had met someone who found Nursery Rhyme Land as fascinating as he did. And, even more unbelievable, liked to listen to him talk about it.

He picked them up. He could see why she'd

called them clown's trousers. They were big and baggy. They looked like a furry jigsaw puzzle.

'These are –' he began proudly. But tiny alarm bells began to ring in his brain. He liked this girl. She seemed a highly intelligent child. She was obviously on his side. But, out of the blue, he remembered Liam's warning, 'Sometimes, Grandad, you're your own worst enemy.' And at the last moment, he decided to choose his words carefully.

'Er, they're very ancient trousers. They probably belonged to one of my ancestors, who owned this place.'

'They're made out of cats, aren't they?' asked Jessica, her little eyes glittering, her pen poised over her notebook. Suddenly, she didn't sound quite so polite.

'No!' laughed Grandad uneasily. 'No! Hot ding! Whatever gave you that idea? Made out of cats? They're rat skin. Yes, that's what they are – rat skin.'

Jessica smiled and said nothing. But in her

notebook she wrote, 'A ginger rat? A stripy rat? I don't think so!'

Gotcha, she thought happily. There was the tiniest twist of unease deep, deep in her mind. But she ignored it.

Grandad was happy too. He rolled the trousers up into a tight bundle and put them back on the crate. He thought he'd handled that pretty well. Got himself out of a sticky situation. He was getting good at this PR business.

'I'll tell you about Grandpa Clamp, shall I?' he said. 'He started this place. Now he was a really interesting man. Actually, today is a very special day in Nursery Rhyme Land. It's the one hundredth anniversary of the day he died.'

Jessica's eyes followed him carefully as he strode about, explaining about Grandpa Clamp. 'Of course, he didn't do it alone. He had an apprentice called Rabbit. Now that's a really sad story.'

When his back was turned she made a nifty dash for the trousers and shoved them under her jacket. They were evidence. She could see them now, in a colour photo, above her article. They might even make the front page. Or the *We Point the Finger!* section on page two, where they named and shamed the town's biggest villains.

She'd got her scoop. No need to hang around this dump any longer. Dad would be really pleased. He'd have to make time to see her now.

Suddenly, she noticed again how creepy it was in there. All those dead creatures dressed as people. Jessica shivered, despite herself. She thought, This place deserves to be destroyed. And once the whole town knew he wore cat-skin trousers, Mr Clamp wouldn't dare open up anywhere else. There'd be riots! Yes, Nursery Rhyme Land was finished, for ever.

I'm doing the world a big favour, thought Jessica uneasily. As well as making her dad notice her.

Tinkle, tinkle.

'What's that?' she said, her eyes shooting round.

But Grandad was still pacing up and down in full flow. He hadn't heard her. 'This place gets a grip on you,' he was saying. 'You can *feel* the history. If these animals could talk, what stories they would tell!'

Jessica snatched up her note pad. She had to escape. She couldn't stay here a moment longer.

'I'm off now,' she said to Grandad.

Grandad paused. He looked surprised and disappointed. 'But you haven't seen my frying-pan arrows yet,' he said. 'Or General Custer's false teeth.'

He knew, of course, that they weren't General Custer's. But he couldn't help pretending that they were. It was the showman in him. Besides, it made such a good story. And he was just revving up to talk about the Wild West when Jessica said again, 'No, I've got to go.'

Please yourself, thought Grandad as she scurried out. But all the same, he thought things had gone rather well. 'Another satisfied customer,' he told himself.

Then he noticed something.

The little stand where General Custer's false teeth had rested was empty. He stared blankly at it. He thought, My memory's getting really rusty. He couldn't for the life of him think where he'd had them last.

'Now where have those blasted teeth got to?' he asked himself, beginning to search for them round Nursery Rhyme Land.

Chapter Five

'I was looking for something else,' Grandad explained to Liam, 'when I noticed my trousers were missing.'

Liam had just arrived. He was red-faced and puffed out. He had skated so fast he'd scorched the pavements. Sparks had flown like fireflies from his wheels.

'I suppose she must have taken them,' sighed Grandad, looking bewildered. He didn't want to believe it. But he had to admit it was the only explanation.

'Course it was her!' said Liam, gasping. 'Grandad, how can you be so trusting?'

It occurred to Liam, not for the first time, what a strange bloke Grandad was. He was wily in some things, innocent in others. He'd been stuck so long in Nursery Rhyme Land he'd forgotten how sneaky the world can be. He'd forgotten that even kids can be sneaky! That made it really hard work trying to protect him.

'I just told you,' said Liam. 'She's a Porteous. Her gran is president of APUP. Her dad edits the paper. And she's ace at finding bad news.'

He didn't explain about Mum, or Snowdrop the fainting goat. It would just make things too complicated.

'Oh dear,' said Grandad vaguely, 'I think I let slip some rather rude things about that Mrs Porteous –'

'Like what?'

'I just said, "That woman has a gob as big as the Channel Tunnel." Still, I don't think Jessica heard me –'

'Oh no,' groaned Liam. 'Grandad, I told you, didn't I? You've got to stop shooting your mouth off. There are people out there who want your head on a plate! Why do you make it easy for them? What a mess!'

But then Grandad said something that made Liam realize that the mess was much more serious than he'd thought.

'There's one good thing,' said Grandad brightly. 'I've just remembered where I put General Custer's false teeth. They were in the pocket of those trousers she nicked.'

A hand seemed to squeeze Liam's heart. A feeling very like *doom* chilled his mind.

'We have to get those trousers back, Grandad,' said Liam frantically. 'We have to get them back, right NOW!'

Grandad couldn't see the need for panic. 'All this fuss about a pair of cat-skin trousers,' he said.

Liam had already told Grandad about the bad publicity. Now he wondered whether to tell him the whole truth: that the trousers and teeth seemed to have some strange and terrible power to unlock the past, and bring Rabbit back into the body of whoever was wearing them.

He even started to tell him. 'Grandad, you know that apprentice of Great Great Great Grandpa Clamp? The one called Rabbit? There's something you ought to know –'

'I was just talking about him to Jessica,' recalled Grandad. 'I hardly know anything about him really. Just snippets, passed down in family stories. He was a mysterious character. A dark horse. No one knew for certain where he came from. Now, what were you going to tell me?'

But Liam didn't answer. He'd just had a startling thought. Grandad was a showman. He liked faking things – he'd faked General Custer's teeth, hadn't he? What if this Rabbit episode was another of his fakes? Something he'd dreamed up in a last desperate effort to pull in the punters?

Liam couldn't imagine why he hadn't thought of it before. It was the obvious explanation.

I bet he was practising on me, thought Liam, half-angry, half-impressed. The old conman. You've got to hand it to him though; it was a pretty good trick. I was nearly wetting my pants! I thought Rabbit had really come back!

He didn't want to tell Grandad right away that he'd rumbled his little game. Let him think that he, Liam, had been taken in. It wouldn't do any harm. And it might give Grandad one tiny thing to feel good about on a day when everything else looked black.

Liam felt himself relaxing a bit. It didn't seem so urgent now to rescue the trousers. Not if the whole thing had been some kind of trick. Mind you, he still had to get them back somehow. Grandad was already the man people loved to loathe. He already had a reputation as a cat hater. Once news of those cat-skin trousers got out, no one would have a kind word to say about him.

'And that would be awful,' murmured Liam. It upset him when people said bad things about Grandad. He took it really personally. Cos he's a nice guy underneath, thought Liam. They just don't understand him.

Grandad was looking all dreamy. 'Do you know,' he told Liam, 'I've had some really good times in Nursery Rhyme Land. After the war, kiddies used to queue up to come in here. They thought this was a magic place. They loved the weasel's bike and the silver tea set and the little

chiming clock in Hickory Dickory
Dock. And all the animals' costumes.
They used to spend hours watching me mending
things. There was no hurry then, no rush.'

'Times have changed, Grandad,' said Liam
impatiently.

'Too right, son,' sighed Grandad, shaking
his head.

'Anyway,' said Liam, trying to sound cheery,
'I'm off to get your trousers back.'

'How?' said Grandad.

'I'll think of something,' said Liam. Even
though, at this moment, he hadn't an idea in his
head. 'I won't be long,' he told Grandad.

'I've got your camera here,' said Grandad,
taking it off a shelf.

'Oh, right, might as well take it with me,' said
Liam, slinging it over his shoulder.

'I'll hold the fort here,' said Grandad. It felt
like Custer's Last Stand. But he couldn't just
surrender. Nursery Rhyme Land deserved more
than that. And anyway, even if the building
got flattened he had to save the display cases.

For Liam's sake.

'You don't have to stay here tonight,' he told Liam.

'I might as well,' said Liam. 'Dad's away until next Wednesday. And Mum's really busy at work. And anyway, I want to.'

'Good lad,' said Grandad, sounding really grateful.

Good job he doesn't know what I *really* feel about Nursery Rhyme Land, thought Liam. It'd probably finish him off.

After Liam had gone, Grandad sat down on the crate. He should be packing up, getting ready to move out tomorrow. But he hadn't the heart. He sank his head in his hands.

Bong, bong.

What was that? It was the clock in the Hickory Dickory Dock case beginning to chime the hour. It shouldn't be doing that. He hadn't wound it up this morning. He got up to have a look. As he passed The Three Little Kittens case, he took a startled step backwards.

'What the –?'

The glass front of the case was shattered. It was still in one piece, but it was a spider's web of cracks. As if someone had been trying to break in.

Grandad knew it was Grandpa Clamp's anniversary – the night when weird things happened in Nursery Rhyme Land. But as he inspected the damaged case it didn't occur, even to him, that someone hadn't been trying to break in. They'd been trying to break out!

Chapter Six

Liam looked at his watch. It was six o'clock. From across the road he could hear the sea sighing and slushing over pebbles. But he couldn't see it. It was already getting dark.

He was crouched outside Mrs Porteous's bungalow, in the bushes just under her window. She must be at home. Her big Hummer, that monster ex-military jeep, was parked in the drive.

Liam's stomach was clenched up with hunger. He could smell the fried onions from the hot-dog stand. But he was more nervous than hungry. He wasn't used to all this sneaking around. He felt like a peeping tom. What if he got caught?

At least he'd located the trousers. But that was his only piece of luck so far. He couldn't get at them. They were hanging on the back of a chair in Mrs Porteous's bedroom.

There was no sign of Jessica. Maybe she'd left them at her grandma's and gone back home for tea.

He thought he'd located the teeth too. There were some in a glass on the bedside table. But then he realized they weren't Rabbit's springy, yellow buck-teeth, but gleaming white modern gnashers.

Rabbit's teeth must still be in the trouser pocket, he thought, shifting his cramped legs. He couldn't help calling them Rabbit's teeth, even though he'd already decided they were no more Rabbit's teeth than they were General Custer's. That was just another of Grandad's stories.

He was beginning to think, What am I doing here? when something happened.

Mrs Porteous came into her bedroom in a big white Stetson hat. Several cats came with her, twisting and twining round her legs.

She came over to the window and yanked the curtains shut. Liam sank out of sight, alarmed.

But she did something else too. She opened the window a crack to let some air in. Cautiously, Liam poked his head over the sill. There was a gap in the curtains he could see through. He could also hear sounds from inside. And what he heard was the *clink, clink, clink* of the spurs on Mrs Porteous's cowgirl boots. They were snazzy two-tone boots, made out of lizard skin.

What Liam didn't know was that Mrs Porteous was all dressed up to go to her American line-dancing class. And that there was an almighty struggle going on inside her. She looked longingly at the cat-skin trousers. Although Grandad didn't know it, she was also a Wild West fanatic. She had bookshelves full of photos of the Old West. She was passionate about getting her costumes right. And in one of her photos was a picture of a gun-totin' cowgirl who wore a pair of buckskin trousers that looked very much like these.

'No, no,' said the angel in Mrs Porteous's mind. 'You can't try those on. You are the president of APUP! Think of the poor little pussies! You should burn these *Trousers of Shame*. Make a bonfire of them!'

'No one need know,' whispered the little devil in honeyed tones. 'Go on, you *know* you want to. Just slip them on. Have a peek at yourself in the mirror. There's no harm in that, is there? You'll look *divine*.'

Mrs Porteous was still undecided. She bent down to scratch behind the ears of one of her pet cats. It purred like a Rolls-Royce engine.

Despite her steely gaze and scary manner, Mrs Porteous had a warm and generous heart – especially where cats were concerned. Her bungalow was open house to all friendless, homeless moggies. She welcomed them all in. She never turned one away.

Shall I? Shan't I? she debated with herself as Liam listened outside.

Her fingers hovered over the tempting trousers. After all, it hadn't been *definitely* proved they were cat-skin. They could be raccoon or squirrel or marmoset. Mrs Porteous secretly fancied herself as a cowgirl, roping steers, *yippy, ki yaying* across the plains.

'*I've got spurs that jingle, jangle, jingle,*' sang Mrs Porteous as she gazed lovingly at the trousers.

She couldn't hold out any longer. She pounced on the trousers and, before Liam's appalled gaze, tugged off her boots and hauled them on.

At least Liam didn't have to cover his eyes. Mrs Porteous was wearing a fringed cowgirl skirt. To his relief, she modestly put the trousers on under it, then took off her skirt.

Phew, thought Liam, wiping his forehead. That was a lucky escape. I could have had a nasty shock.

Mrs Porteous would make two, maybe three, of Liam's skinny grandad. The trousers that were baggy on him were a very snug fit on her. But she liked them that way.

She twirled in front of the mirror, admiring herself from all angles. She snapped the brim of her enormous Stetson hat. The spurs on her cowgirl boots jangle-jingled every time she moved.

Then she stopped turning. Liam found himself staring for five minutes at her multi-coloured bottom.

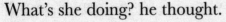

What's she doing? he thought.

She seemed to be fumbling in her trouser pocket. Dreadful suspicions reared up like cobras in Liam's mind. But the cats knew something was wrong before he did. Fur bristling like hedgehogs, they'd shot off into all four corners of the room. Shivering, they peeped out from under the chairs.

Oh no, Liam thought. This isn't happening.

He leaped up from his hiding place and yelled a frantic warning. 'No! Don't put those teeth in!' He slung his camera round his neck for extra safety. Then, in one nimble move, he pushed the window wide open and vaulted through into the bedroom. 'Mrs Porteous!'

Too late. Rabbit's belongings, his teeth and trousers, had exerted their sinister power.

Mrs Porteous was fitting his teeth into her jaw. Cramming them in with both hands, like a baby stuffing itself with chocolate.

'*Clack, clack.*' She tried out the teeth. '*Clack clack.*'

Liam couldn't see her face yet. But he knew what was coming by those suddenly stooping shoulders. Mrs Porteous always stalked around as if she had an iron corset on. Now Liam *had* to believe what was happening. For, when she finally turned round, the expression on her face wasn't stern and super-confident. It was a cringing, beaten-puppy look.

'I come as quick as I could,' a familiar, whining voice came out of Mrs Porteous's mouth.

He's back! thought Liam, horrified.

It hadn't been Grandad putting on an act. It had been Rabbit all along.

'May God 'elp me!' wailed Rabbit, looking down at himself. He sounded absolutely aghast. 'There's only so much a poor boy can stand! Whose body 'ave I come back in this time?'

Liam was too shocked to reply. He just asked in a stunned voice, 'Who are you?'

The teeth weren't a perfect fit. They slopped around in Mrs Porteous's mouth. When Rabbit spoke again they clacked and they hissed like an angry snake.

'*Clack.* I fort I *told* yer. *Sssss.*' Rabbit's voice hissed on as in a dream. 'I catched crows for a farmer and the fields was black and freezing. Me hands was all swoll up with the cold! And me dad he gets drunk near every night. So I runs away and I gets sent up chimneys. It's all black up there too. Black and hot. Me knees and elbows is all scabbed! So I runs away, I gets brought back. I gets beat black and blue. I runs away again. I gets very low. I goes collecting dog dung for the leather tanners. *Clack*.'

'Beg pardon?' said Liam, dazed.

'Are you deaf or somefing? Dog dung! What tanners use to make the leather soft. But I loses that job and they says, "It's the work'ouse for the likes of you, me lad." So I runs away and sells me teef to buy a hunk of bread.'

'Sells your teef?' repeated Liam, like a robot.

'Course! I gets 'em all took out. They was loose in any case. But it were still agony!' Rabbit paused to admire Mrs Porteous's line-dancing boots. '*Sssss*. These are tremenjous boots,' he said. 'What they made of?'

He can't half talk, thought Liam, whose fuddled brain was just starting to clear.

But Rabbit hadn't finished his life story.

'*Clack*. Me teef gets made into false 'uns and this toff buys 'em. So I follows this geezer. I keeps my eye on him. And he's just about to sink me teef into a lamb chop when I nicks 'em back.'

Rabbit couldn't miss Liam's open-mouthed, astonished stare.

'I just swipes 'em out his mouf. Well, what would you have done? Anyways, this toff calls the police. And, would you credit it, I nearly gets arrested for nicking me own teef. That's not blooming right, is it?'

Liam shook his head dumbly.

'Then me teef money runs out, I gets awful low again. I can't even get work shovelling dog dung. Me clothes is rags. Me hands, they look like skellington's bones.' Here, Rabbit glanced down at Mrs Porteous's plump hands and her gold rings, as big as knuckle-dusters, with some surprise. 'Then me master finds me, Mr Clamp. He says to himself, "That boy looks sharp!" He takes me in, he fills me belly, he gives me these trousers, he gives me work. I don't have to run away no more.

I'm finking, Rabbit, you're in heaven!'

After his first shock, Liam found himself actually listening. It wasn't half as freaky as he'd feared – looking at Mrs Porteous and listening to Rabbit. He was actually beginning to get used to it. Even though Rabbit had been dead for over a hundred years.

'What work did you do for my Great Great Great Grandpa Clamp?' asked Liam.

'I was his cat-catcher,' said Rabbit. 'I was very good at it. On account of practising with crows.'

Liam felt that icy grip clutch his heart. He'd just started to feel sorry for Rabbit, with his drunken dad and scabby knees and swollen hands – and ever-empty belly. Liam was thinking, He had a terrible life. And now Rabbit was telling him that he caught cats for Grandpa Clamp. Cats that ended up stuffed inside glass cases! He felt his sympathy gush away, like water down a plughole.

'What happened to the poor cats?' asked Liam. He had a pretty good idea. But he still dreaded the answer.

'That was Master's business,' said Rabbit. 'I

never did it. But it was quick. And they was doomed anyway. They was strays. They would've starved to death in the gutter. It was a kindness really.'

'A kindness!' roared Liam, shaking with outrage.

He felt bitterly ashamed of his cruel Great Great Great Grandpa. How awful, having a cat-killer in the family! Even if it was so long ago. But he couldn't forgive Rabbit either. He thought, He shouldn't have been a cat-catcher. There's no excuse! I wouldn't have done it. I would've said, 'No way!'

A cat came slinking out from under a chair. It was a scraggy black cat, the latest homeless moggy that Mrs Porteous had rescued. It was devoted to Mrs Porteous. It could never stay away from its mistress for long.

The cat sniffed at the cowgirl boots, then suddenly arched its backbone, spitting like fury.

'Here, kitty, kitty,' said Rabbit. 'Now where's me sack?'

He pounced, quick as lightning. The cat

howled, *'Yeow!'* and shot up the curtains.

Rabbit stalked it. Mrs Porteous's body wasn't very good for stalking. In his own body, back in the nineteenth century, Rabbit had been quick and slippery as an eel. But this body was clumsier, much slower. Its joints were creaky. It was really cramping his style.

'Drat! Missed it,' said Rabbit, looking up at the black cat trembling on the curtain rail.

'No!' said Liam, appalled. 'Leave it alone. You're not cat-hunting now!'

But something strange had happened. The returned spirit of Rabbit was in cat-hunting mode. Its eyes gleamed like a killer shark. It remembered, This is what I was good at. This is what made Master proud of me.

'Here's me sack!' said Rabbit.

He picked up a Tesco carrier bag that was lying on the bed. 'I'm off cat-catching, cat-catching, cat-catching,' he chanted.

Then Rabbit walked Mrs Porteous's body out of the bedroom, down the hall, out the back door and into the garden.

Liam stared after the retreating Stetson with horrified disbelief. The clink of cowgirl boots faded into the distance.

He heard a faint, 'Here, kitty, kitty.' Then silence.

'Get after him, no, *her*!' Liam's brain screamed at him. It gave him two reasons:

1 To save innocent kitties from being cat-
 napped.

2 To snap lots of photos.

Shocked as he was, it hadn't escaped Liam's notice that this was a once-in-a-lifetime photo opportunity. Mrs Porteous, the president of APUP, out in cat-skin trousers, hunting kittens. That's what it would *look* like anyway. It was about time APUP got some bad press – they had been dishing the dirt on Grandad long enough. And, thought Liam, some incriminating snaps might give him something to bargain with.

You've got to be as sneaky as Jessica, he excused himself. Fight her with her own weapons.

But thinking was wasting time. He got his

camera out the case. Then he was off, in hot pursuit of Rabbit in his borrowed body. He was just in time to see Rabbit, with his Tesco carrier bag, heaving Mrs Porteous's body over the garden wall.

Liam shouted, 'Come back.'

But there was no use talking to Rabbit now. Liam couldn't control him. Rabbit was repeating actions he'd done a hundred times in the past. He was bringing the booty home to Grandpa Clamp. And Grandpa Clamp would grab the writhing sack, pat him on the head and say, 'Rabbit, you're the best apprentice a master could have.'

Liam rushed through the moonlit garden, scrambled over the wall and dropped into an alley. It was very dark here. A prime prowling ground for cats. Black pools of spooky shadow were everywhere.

He looked frantically up and down. Where was Rabbit?

Then he heard him, '*Sssss*. Here, kitty, kitty. I got some sardines. *Clack*.'

Liam thought, He's found one. He tried to stay

cool. 'Take the photo first,' his brain told him. '*Then* rescue the cat.'

He held his camera ready. It would flash automatically. He just hoped his batteries hadn't run down.

He crept through the darkness. Saw a black bulky shape ahead, tiptoeing stealthily down the alley. That's them, he thought, as if Rabbit the cat-catcher and Mrs Porteous, president of APUP, were in league together.

A sound rang through the silence: *Clink! Clink! Yowl!* He never even saw the cat. He only heard the clangs as, startled, it shot off among some empty dustbins.

'Drat these clinking boots,' he heard Rabbit say. 'They ain't no good at all for cat-catching.'

Then Rabbit did something that Liam hadn't planned for. He walked out of the dark alley on to the sea front, where the street lights lit up everything in a bright yellow glow. Liam lurked in the shadows, reluctant to follow. He peeped out. Mrs Porteous's bungalow and Nursery Rhyme Land were just a few steps down the road.

'This'll be good,' chuckled Liam.

He even wondered about running to fetch Grandad so he could watch too. But then thought better of it. He had to get that photo.

He followed Rabbit, trying to look casual, but prepared to take a snap at any moment. He was pleased to see that there were plenty of evening strollers, walking their dogs. They would be witnesses. And there, right on cue, rubbing itself against a lamp post, was a pretty white cat with a blue collar round its neck. It was obviously someone's precious pet.

Liam grinned. He could hardly believe his luck. Everything's perfect, he thought.

What he didn't know was that Rabbit had spotted something on the pavement. It took his mind off cats altogether. It made him remember an even earlier job. The one he'd had before Grandpa Clamp rescued him.

'Here's me sack,' murmured Rabbit. 'But where's me shovel?'

Liam saw Mrs Porteous slowly bending down –
With one glance, he'd sized up the situation.

Oh no, he thought. I don't believe it! He's dog-dung collecting now! Yuk! He's not going to pick that up!

But even Rabbit wasn't that disgusting. He used his Tesco bag to scoop it up. Then looked around for some more.

Why isn't he *cat-catching*? thought Liam, gritting his teeth in frustration. It was a total disaster. His plans had backfired.

The people on the sea front looked on with approval. What they saw was the formidable Mrs Porteous, on her way to line-dancing class, pausing to clean up the town's pavements. Some of the dog walkers looked especially guilty.

'That woman!' said a passer-by. 'What a good citizen! How public spirited is that? She puts us all to shame!' People even clapped, to show their appreciation. 'She deserves a medal! I'm going to write to the newspaper this very night and say so!'

Liam gave a long, hopeless sigh. Things had suddenly gone pear-shaped. This was the exact opposite of what was supposed to happen.

He felt like leaping out the alley, pointing

dramatically and shouting, 'Hey! Use your eyes! She might be doing a good job scooping poop, but she's wearing *cat-skin* kegs!' But he was a naturally shy boy. He couldn't bring himself to do it.

Then things took a turn for the better. To Liam's relief, Mrs Porteous's body did a stealthy turn and disappeared down another alleyway.

'Great!' murmured Liam. 'Rabbit's cat-catching again.'

He couldn't understand it. In ghost stories, spirits that rose from the dead weren't this irritating. They were reassuringly predictable. They haunted the same place, did the same spooky thing for years on end. They didn't go mucking you about, switching from one thing to another like Rabbit was doing.

Liam thought, I've *got* to get my photo this time.

To make sure he didn't miss his chance, he followed right on Rabbit's heels, as close as his shadow. He almost brushed off the big white Stetson. Every second, he thought Rabbit would turn round and spot him. But Rabbit didn't even notice. He seemed to be circling back towards Mrs Porteous's bungalow.

Miaow!

Excellent! thought Liam, raising the camera.

Rabbit had found a cat. He seemed to be able to sniff them out. He was the best cat-finder in the world, ever. He forced Mrs Porteous's body into a running crouch. Her knee joints cracked like gunshot.

'Shut up, shut up,' Rabbit told his borrowed body.

Two golden eyes glowed in the dark. A security light snapped on behind a pub. It flooded the scene. And Liam saw a tiny, scared kitten, with tiger stripes all over its body.

Oh no, thought Liam. What should he do now? He was torn in two. He wanted that photo. But how far should he let Rabbit go? He didn't want him to grab the kitten and stuff it inside that Tesco bag. He hadn't forgotten what was in there already.

I'll let him grab it, thought Liam. Then I'll grapple with him!

It occurred to him that he'd be grappling with the ample bod of Mrs Porteous. But his head couldn't cope with that. Some things just can't be imagined –

So he raised his camera. 'Fantastic,' he breathed. 'Here, kitty, kitty.'

Its eyes like saucers, the tiny cat moved closer and closer. Mrs Porteous's head moved from side to side. Rabbit seemed to be hypnotizing his victim like a snake.

Quick as a flash, Rabbit sprang.

Miaow!

Plump white hands, chunky with rings, were round the cat's neck. This was just what Liam wanted. He took the damning picture. It was perfect. There was more than enough light to see every detail.

Now he had to move quickly. But first he zipped his camera away. Must be sure it was safe. That photo was more precious than gold.

Then he lowered his head and charged at Mrs Porteous's body like a little bull. It seemed the only thing to do, at the time.

'*Oof!*' she gasped, as he hit her in the midriff and Rabbit's teeth flew out of her mouth.

With admirable cool, Liam caught them – a brilliant, one-handed catch – and stuffed them in his pocket. He gave a joyful shout, 'Bye bye, Rabbit!'

The kitten had escaped, scuttled off into the dark. The Tesco carrier bag had dropped to the ground. Liam left it there. He'd always been taught to pick up litter. But he thought he'd give it a miss, just this once.

He stared around, trying to collect his scattered wits. They were outside Mrs Porteous's back garden. There was a gate in her wall that Liam hadn't noticed before. It was opening. Jessica came out.

'Granny!' she said. 'I was looking all over for you. What are you doing out here in Mr Clamp's trousers?'

Liam slipped away, like the tiger-striped cat, into the dark. He hadn't planned on meeting Jessica quite so soon. He needed more time to think ...

*

Meanwhile, back at the university, things were going from bad to worse. As Liam's mum had predicted, local telly had got hold of the story. They were camped outside with a big van and cameras. She felt she was under siege. The loyal Milton had stayed behind to support her. He was in the lab, polishing his famous teeth collection.

At least I don't have to worry about Liam, Mum thought. He's safe with his grandad.

For a moment, she thought regretfully about Grandad. She wished they were closer. How had they drifted so far apart? These days, they almost seemed like strangers –

Suddenly, she peered outside. She'd seen something. It was seven o' clock and already dark, but the moonlight made it almost as bright as day. She tapped angrily on the window.

'Milton!' she yelled. 'That pesky kid is back again!'

Faithful Milton came bounding out of the lab. He too peered out the window. It was the same kid as before. Only this time, he'd brought a little friend.

Unaware they were being watched, they tiptoed along the side of the building. They seemed to know exactly where they were going.

Milton rushed along the corridor, heading for the EXIT door. He was trying to head them off.

But the two kids had already reached Snowdrop's pen. Snowdrop wasn't asleep yet. She had no idea, of course, of the sensation she'd caused. She didn't know she was headline news. She was full of the joys of life, innocently skipping about in the silvery moonbeams.

She didn't see the boys as they crept closer, keeping in the shadow of the wall.

'Watch this,' hissed the boy who'd been there before.

He crawled right up to the pen on all fours. Sucked in a deep breath. Then leaped up like a jack-in-the-box.

'BOO!' he yelled.

Whump. Snowdrop keeled over in a dead faint.

'It works every time!' said the boy delightedly

to his friend. And they both dashed off, giggling themselves silly.

From inside her office, Liam's mum watched the boys scoot away like hares. Where was Milton? He'd never catch them now.

'Seven, eight, nine, ten,' she counted. Snowdrop scrambled to her feet just as Milton came crashing through the EXIT door. *Whump*. There she goes again. Liam's mum sighed and shook her head. She knew the local kids would be back. They just couldn't resist it. Probably a whole gang of them next time.

That poor goat, she thought. She's just too highly strung! She can't stay here any longer. She needs someone to look after her. Someone with loads of patience.

Now who do I know like that? she thought. But sadly, she couldn't think of anyone.

Chapter Seven

Liam nipped over the garden wall and dived into the bushes in Mrs Porteous's garden. He'd got Rabbit's teeth, but he hadn't got his trousers. He'd promised Grandad. He wasn't going back to Nursery Rhyme Land without them.

He watched Jessica lead her gran gently back into the bungalow.

'What's going on?' Mrs Porteous kept asking in a helpless, bewildered voice.

Liam had a lot of sympathy with that question. He'd asked it himself a hundred times since this Rabbit business began.

He let ten minutes go by. Then he crept up to the bedroom window. He peeped through the gap in the curtains. There was only a dim light inside the room. He could just make out Mrs Porteous lying flat out on her bed. Her Stetson had fallen off and she was pressing a packet of frozen peas to her forehead.

I expect she's got a bit of a headache, thought Liam.

The problem was, she still had the trousers on. How was he ever going to get his hands on them now? Except he had something to trade. He had the photo of Mrs Porteous, president of the Association for the Prevention of Unkindness to Pussies, wearing cat skin and apparently strangling a kitten.

But he had to pluck up his courage first. Mrs Porteous was in a collapsed state. It was no good trying to do a deal with her. That meant he would have to do business with Jessica. Just the thought of that gave him the jitters. He had the idea that she could be a *very* slippery customer.

I hope she doesn't remember my joke about school custard, he thought nervously.

He looked through the window again. Mrs

Porteous's devoted black cat approached cautiously. It sniffed the air. Then it leaped on to the bed miaowing, as if to welcome its mistress back. It didn't seem to mind that she was wearing trousers made of its fellow moggies.

Liam circled the house. Jessica was in the living room, watching telly. He took a deep breath.

'It's no use putting this off,' he told himself, sternly.

He went up to the front door. Rang the bell. DING DONG. The ring sounded loud and confident. But Liam was thinking, What am I doing here? He didn't even have a proper plan. He would have to play things by ear.

Jessica came to the door and opened it a crack. She said, 'Yes?'

Phew! thought Liam, I don't think she recognizes me.

Then she said, 'I know you! You go to my school. You called custard yellow dog-sick.'

Oh great! thought Liam with an inward groan. Along with all her other talents, she obviously had a perfect memory. It didn't make him feel any braver.

Words he hadn't planned rushed out
of his mouth. 'You wrote about my mum!' he said.
'*FREAKY FAINTING GOAT FIASCO AT
FRANKENSTEIN LAB.* Remember? Well, my
mum works in that lab. You've caused lots of
trouble!'

Even as he spoke he was thinking, Why am I
talking like this? I didn't come to talk about Mum.

'Oh, is that what you're here for,' said Jessica
calmly. 'Well, I just wrote the truth. I wrote what I
saw. Don't blame me.'

Liam struggled to get his mind on the right
track. He was in danger of going to pieces here.
'Get a grip,' he ordered himself. 'Concentrate on
the *trousers*.'

He gulped once, twice. His next words came
out in a desperate yell. 'You nicked Grandad's
trousers! And he wants them back!'

Again, Jessica didn't seem at all put out. Being
fingered as a trouser thief didn't bother her one
bit.

'I didn't know Mr Clamp was your grandad,'

she said. 'You kept quiet about that, didn't you? Anyway, the public have a right to know what he's really like. And those trousers are evidence.'

It was no use pleading with her that she'd got Grandad all wrong, thought Liam. That he didn't have horns and a tail. She seemed to have already made up her mind about him.

Using bully-boy tactics didn't come naturally to Liam. He hated violence and threats. So he said, almost apologetically, 'Well, in that case, er, I don't want you to think this is blackmail or anything, but I've got a photo of your granny being cruel to a kitten. And if you don't give me those trousers I'm going to put it on the World Wide Web.'

'Come in,' said Jessica, yanking him through the door.

She led him through to the living room. 'My gran's poorly,' explained Jessica. 'She's got one of her heads.'

I'm not surprised, thought Liam. He felt quite sorry for Mrs Porteous. No wonder she felt rough. Grandad hadn't felt too great either after Rabbit had borrowed his body. And Rabbit hadn't taken *him* out dog-dung collecting and cat-catching.

'Where is this photo then?' demanded Jessica. She was a suspicious person. But now her eyes narrowed even more, as if she didn't trust Liam one little bit.

'Here,' said Liam. He unpacked his digital camera and showed her the little viewing screen at the back. 'Your gran,' he said, 'is a secret cat strangler.' He didn't sound very convincing, even to himself.

Jessica peered at the tiny screen. 'Wait a minute,' she said. 'That could be anyone under that Stetson! It could even be your grandad, trying to set my grandma up!'

Liam thought this was unlikely, since Grandad looked like a string bean and Mrs Porteous like a barrage balloon. But he'd got the message. I should have checked that photo before, he thought hopelessly. The big white Stetson seemed to fill the screen. She's right. It could be anyone!

He took a deep, deep breath. There was only

one thing for it. Tell the truth. Jessica was tapping the photo impatiently. Her sharp, questioning eyes were watching him with hawk-like concentration.

'Look,' said Liam, 'I don't want those trousers back just to protect my grandad. I know this sounds crazy, but those trousers are dangerous. They're a really bad influence. And when you fit in *these* false teeth,' like a magician he whipped Rabbit's yellow buck-teeth out of his pocket, 'it's a deadly combination!'

Jessica didn't look impressed. In fact, she stared at him as if he'd totally lost the plot.

I'm not making a very good job of this, thought Liam. He *had* to make her understand. He was driven to even more desperate measures. He would give her a quick demo. He didn't want to do it. It was risky, it meant recalling Rabbit one more time. But he felt he had no choice. It was the quickest way to make her believe him.

'I'll show you,' he said.

'Hey,' said Jessica. 'You can't go in there. It's Grandma's bedroom.'

'Look,' said Liam, 'I know we're supposed to be

on different sides. But I'm trying to help *my* grandad and *your* grandma. Right?'

Jessica was just eleven years old. But she was good at sniffing out liars, and she didn't think Liam was lying. He seemed to be seriously concerned. She didn't have a clue what he was raving on about, but she decided to humour him, just for the moment.

Mrs Porteous was lying on her bed – still looking the worse for wear. The frozen peas were pressed to her forehead. The cat-skin trousers clashed terribly with her flowery duvet.

Liam had a moment's stomach-churning doubt. What am I doing here? he thought. So many mind-boggling things had happened since teatime. If someone had told him, just this morning, that by tonight he'd be trying to summon up the spirit of Grandpa Clamp's cat-catcher – well, he'd have looked at them just like Jessica was looking at him now: as if he needed his head examining.

He gritted his own teeth while grasping Rabbit's teeth firmly in his hand, and strode across the shadowy room.

'Who are you?' said Mrs Porteous, in a dazed voice. 'You're not Jessica.'

As she spoke, Liam gazed into her open mouth, as pink and gummy as a baby's and thought, *Yuk*, I can't do this.

He didn't have to. The teeth had a magnetic attraction. Mrs Porteous snatched them greedily out of Liam's hand and, *gulp*, seemed to swallow them whole. Her face twitched and jerked into that familiar hangdog look. She cringed back against the headboard.

Clack. Sssss, went the teeth as Rabbit prepared to talk. Yellow buck-teeth protruded and rested on Mrs Porteous's bottom lip. Whoever had made that false set out of Rabbit's real teeth hadn't done a very good job.

'That's not my gran!' said Jessica.

Yowl! The black cat bristled as if it had had an electric shock. It stood on tiptoes. Then it did a loop-the-loop and streaked under the wardrobe.

Liam was just as spooked. He searched in his mouth for spit. But it felt as dry as ashes. This was

the third time he'd seen Rabbit return
from the past. It wasn't something you
got used to. It got creepier every time.

But he wasn't going to allow Rabbit long. He
felt more in control this time. He was going to shut
him up after a few seconds. Just long enough for
Jessica to get the picture.

'Tell – us – who – you – are,' ordered Liam,
slowly and clearly, as if he was talking to a half-
wit.

He nodded at Jessica as if to say, 'Check this
out!' But she looked stunned, like a creature
caught in car headlights.

Clack. You must be the stupidest boy what ever
lived,' complained Rabbit. 'Have you got suet for
brains? I told yer before. I'm *Rabbit,* yer Grandpa
Clamp's apprentice!'

Then Rabbit launched eagerly into his life
story. He had told Liam the main events. He was
filling in the gaps now.

'I always washed me!' he protested, snivelling. 'I
never went to bed sooty black like them other
climbing boys. Yer grandpa said I smelled really

sweet – for a dog-dung collector.'

'This is Jessica,' said Liam, desperately trying to distract him. But it just meant Rabbit had a new audience so he could start all over again.

'Do you know, I nearly got arrested for stealing me own teef?' Rabbit asked her. 'Now ain't that interesting?'

Jessica nodded her head dumbly. It looked as if someone was pulling her strings. Liam remembered that feeling, from the first time that Rabbit came back.

Rabbit was doing some more reminiscing.

'I loved Mr Clamp,' he said. 'He give me these trousers. Did I tell yer that? He was kind to me. He was a real gent. I'd be really proud if he was my granfer.'

Liam made a face. He murmured, 'I'm not proud.'

He'd thought about it. It was a narrow squeak, but he could *just about* forgive Rabbit for cat hunting. He might have done the same if he was a starving wretch in a gutter. But his heart had hardened against Grandpa Clamp. He could never forgive him for being a cat murderer, no matter how kind he'd been to Rabbit. Liam hated Nursery Rhyme Land more than ever now when he thought of its gruesome beginnings.

He didn't want to hear any more praise of Grandpa Clamp. Or anything else about the history of Nursery Rhyme Land. He couldn't handle it. It made him feel sick.

'Shut up, shut up,' groaned Liam as Rabbit rabbited on. He could have kicked himself for bringing him back. He was sure Jessica had heard enough.

Then, in the dim glow of the bedside lamp, Mrs Porteous's body started to move. Rabbit didn't like these creaky old limbs. But they were better than nothing. He might as well give them a try-out.

'No!' cried Liam. 'You've got to stay here.'

'Who do you fink you are, telling me what to do?' said Rabbit. 'You're not my master.'

And Mrs Porteous's cowgirl boots swung chinking to the floor.

Rabbit was out of control. What if he took Mrs Porteous's body off cat hunting again? Or tried to shove it up chimneys? It didn't bear thinking about.

'Bring Mrs Porteous back!' said Liam.

'Get lorst!' Rabbit moved resolutely to the door.

To his amazement, Jessica stepped briskly forward. He hadn't expected any back-up from her. He thought she was still in shock.

She thrust her open hand under her gran's chin. 'Spit them out, Gran,' she commanded. 'Spit those false teeth out *now*!'

Mrs Porteous was a strong-minded woman. And somewhere deep, deep down, in a part of her brain that wasn't quite taken over by Rabbit, she heard her granddaughter's voice. Would she, could she, do what it asked?

Rabbit seemed aware of the danger. Once those teeth went, he would be snuffed out again. He would be history. And he still had lots of his story to tell.

'Oi!' He tried teetering away in the cowgirl boots.

If he'd been in his own body, he would have

dodged about, twisted and turned like a leaf in the wind. But he had to use this clapped-out model. It was just one of the disadvantages of being dead.

Jessica headed him off at the door.

'Oi,' whinged Rabbit again. 'Don't take me body away. *Clack.* Have pity, miss, on a miserable fellow creature. I was just going to tell yer all about dog-dung collecting. Now *that's* interesting.'

'Gran!' snapped Jessica. 'Give me those teeth! Now!'

There was a last strangled cry from Rabbit. It sounded as if it was coming from the end of a very long tunnel. Then Mrs Porteous obediently coughed out Rabbit's big yellow tombstone teeth. They sprang smartly on to Jessica's open palm, where they clacked twice. Then were silent.

Solemnly, Jessica handed the teeth to Liam.

'Phew!' said Liam, wiping his forehead. 'That was close. Once he'd got out of that door we might never have got your gran back.'

He put the teeth safely away in the knee pocket of his combat pants. He made sure the flap was buttoned down. 'Phew!' he said again. He felt a little bit better now.

Jessica was busy soothing her befuddled gran: 'It's all right, Gran. It's all right. You just had one of your turns.'

She led her towards the bed. Meek as a lamb, Mrs Porteous climbed under the duvet. It had all been too much for her. She fell instantly asleep. Soon her snores filled the room.

Jessica came back to Liam. 'Poor Gran. I think she'll be all right when she wakes up.'

'See?' said Liam. He couldn't help using his *I-told-you-so* voice. 'That's what I was trying to warn you about.'

'I still don't understand what happened.'

'That was Rabbit, my Great Great Great Grandpa Clamp's apprentice. I've been thinking about it actually,' said Liam, stroking his chin gravely. 'I mean, buildings have ghosts. You see it in scary films on telly. So why not other things, like trousers? Or teeth?'

'Haunted trousers?' said Jessica, raising her eyebrows.

'And the ghosts come back on special occasions. Well, today is a really special occasion. It's Grandpa Clamp's hundredth anniversary.'

'I don't believe in ghosts,' said Jessica firmly.

'Well, I don't know, do I?' said Liam, throwing his arms out helplessly. 'Maybe Rabbit time-travelled back!'

'Now *that* might be scientifically possible,' conceded Jessica.

'But anyway, you saw what happened. It happened to my grandad as well. About an hour ago in Nursery Rhyme Land. I don't know *why* it happens. But some power in those teeth and trousers brings Rabbit back.'

Jessica frowned. 'Then we've got to destroy them,' she said.

There was no question of them being enemies now. This was an emergency. They were working together, for the sake of their grandparents.

Jessica rushed over to the bed and flung the duvet off Mrs Porteous. She tugged off the two-tone lizard-skin boots that Rabbit admired so much. Mrs Porteous's snores still rumbled round the room.

'I'm going to get these trousers off before Gran wakes up. Phew, she's heavy. Can you help me?'

'No way!' Liam backed off, horrified. He seemed destined, before this night was out, to see Mrs Porteous's bloomers. There's only so much a poor boy can stand, he thought, unconsciously echoing Rabbit's words.

There was a great deal of grunting and groaning as Jessica wrestled the trousers off her gran. But, amazingly, Mrs Porteous slumbered on.

'It's OK, I got 'em,' said Jessica, flapping the cat-skin pants like a flag. 'Now what do we do? Cut 'em up or something? There's some scissors in the kitchen drawer.'

'Wait,' said Liam.

Jessica stopped. She turned round, surprised.

Liam gave an apologetic shrug. 'Those trousers and teeth, they belong to my grandad actually. They're his things. He's had them for years.'

'So?' demanded Jessica. 'They're a danger to the public. Well, not to *all* the public,' she admitted. 'Just to toothless old wrinklies.'

Liam flapped his hands in frustration. He was finding it hard to explain. 'Look,' he said, 'my grandad's losing everything tomorrow. Everything he cares about. Nursery Rhyme Land is going to be bulldozed into the ground! I think the trousers and teeth should be destroyed. But I think we should ask him first. I don't want to be like these people that are just taking his things away, things that he's cared about all his life, without even asking him first.'

Liam sighed. He didn't expect any sympathy for Grandad. He took it for granted that Jessica shared Mrs Porteous's point of view. But he was in for a shock.

'OK,' agreed Jessica. That was all she was going to say. But when she saw Liam's look of wonder, she confessed, 'I quite like your grandad. He's all right.'

Liam wanted to demand, So why were you going to write bad things about him? And, another thing, do you know what trouble you caused at the university? My mum's practically having a nervous breakdown!

But he knew this was not the right time. 'We'd better get over to Nursery Rhyme Land,' he said.

'Let's be quick then,' said Jessica. 'I want to get back before Gran wakes up.'

What they didn't know was that Mrs Porteous was already awake. She watched them blearily through one half-open eye. She saw them dash out the door.

Her head was slowly starting to clear. She felt more like her old self again.

Where's Jessica going? she thought. Anxiety made her sit up. And who's that boy with her?

She staggered out of bed and over to the window. To her alarm, she saw two running figures heading for Nursery Rhyme Land. Why is Jessica going into that dreadful place? And at this time of night? she wondered. There was definitely something fishy going on. She determined to follow her granddaughter.

Then she caught sight of herself in the bedroom mirror. I can't go out like this, she thought. People will laugh! So she put on her big white Stetson and fringed cowgirl skirt. She chose another pair from her vast boot collection, rattlesnake skin this time. She put in her own false teeth. She was ready.

Outside on the street, Jessica suddenly stopped running. She was recovering a bit from meeting Rabbit. She was back in reporter mode again. And she wanted to get things clear.

'Look,' she said to Liam, as if she was going to write all this down in her notebook. 'Let's get this straight. We're going to see your grandad, right? Then we're going to get rid of these trousers and teeth for good.'

Liam nodded. He wasn't offended when she wagged her finger at him. He was more relieved than anything. Before Jessica joined him, he felt he was blundering around in a fog. Now they were a team there was a way out. Jessica made it seem easy.

But it wasn't going to be as easy as they thought. They would have realized that if they'd

known what was going on back in Nursery
Rhyme Land.

Chapter Eight

Grandad was up to his scraggy neck in trouble. Things were getting out of hand. He'd always been used to being in charge in Nursery Rhyme Land – like the king of his own little country. If things went wrong he fixed them. Nothing happened without his say-so. But now things were happening all around him that he had no control over at all. There was rebellion in Nursery Rhyme Land.

There'd been warning signs, like the weasel's bike bell and the chiming Hickory Dickory Dock clock. But they were little things. They had happened before, on other anniversaries. And anyway, Grandad could never be sure whether he'd imagined them or not. With all the bad publicity, there had been no visitors to Nursery Rhyme Land for a very long time. In here, all alone day after day, sewing ears on cats, gluing beaks on owls – it was hardly surprising if you started hearing and seeing things.

In fact, Grandad sometimes asked himself, 'Am I going a little bit funny?'

The broken glass on The Three Little Kittens case – he hadn't imagined that. He was staring at it right now. But even that could have been an accident.

The first *really* disturbing thing happened soon after Liam left on his trouser hunt.

Grandad was lighting the candles. Usually, he didn't make a big fuss on Grandpa Clamp's anniversary. But he'd found a dozen fat, white candles in the old wooden chest.

Might as well light them up, he thought. After all, it is the old chap's one hundredth. Candlelight wouldn't harm the fragile exhibits. It was only harsh, brilliant light they couldn't stand.

A soft lemony glow spread round Nursery Rhyme Land. Bizarre shadows danced on the wall.

Bzzzz!

Something batted in Grandad's face.
He swatted at it wildly. What was it? A bee? How did that get in here?

A thin, whiny, buzzing noise came from the ground near his feet. Grandad looked down. I hope it's not hurt, he was thinking. He was about to rescue the bee, put it safely outside –

Until he saw that it had a wedding dress on.

The buzzing stopped.

In a state of shock, Grandad bent down and scooped up the tiny body.

Stunned, he walked over to the smallest display in Nursery Rhyme Land. It was next to Who Killed Cock Robin? The glass case was no bigger than a matchbox. The nursery rhyme next to it said:

> *Fiddle di dee, Fiddle di dee,*
> *The Fly had married the Bumble Bee.*
> *Says the Fly, says he, 'Will you marry me,*
> *Sweet Bumble Bee?'*

Says the Bee, says she,
'I'll live under your wing
And you'll never know I carry a sting.'
Fiddle di dee, Fiddle di dee,
The Fly had married the Bumble Bee.

It was a miracle of craftsmanship. Probably Grandpa Clamp's best work ever. He'd been really good at miniature things, the smaller the better. He could have painted a picture on a rice grain.

You needed a magnifying glass to really appreciate it. The fly bridegroom had a wedding suit on and a top hat, hardly bigger than a match head. But he was all on his own tonight. His little bee bride lay on Grandad's palm, her tiny wings poking through slits in her wedding dress and folded across her back.

There was no mistaking it. It's not every day you see a bee in a wedding dress. And anyway, Grandad knew every stitch on her white frock. Before his eyes got too bad he had spent hours repairing it with almost invisible sewing, trying to keep the delicate silk in one piece.

How on earth did she get out? he thought, his mind a blur of confusion. Then he saw. The wooden back of the case had somehow worked itself loose. There was a tiny gap. Big enough for a bee to crawl through.

'She can't have done that,' Grandad scolded himself. 'Don't be silly.'

It must have been something else he'd swatted. A wasp maybe. They were a menace, always buzzing round the litter bins on the sea front.

The little bee bride lay quite still on his palm. Her body was dried-up and hollow. She was lighter than a cobweb. If you breathed too hard you'd blow her away.

But how *did* she get out? Grandad was really struggling to think of an explanation.

Then a mouse scuttled across the floor. It came from the direction of the Hickory Dickory Dock case. It left a tiny trail of sawdust behind it. But Grandad didn't see that. He didn't have his specs on.

Mice! thought Grandad. He almost laughed out loud with relief. Those pesky varmints get everywhere. They could have chewed their way into the case, dragged her out. And all those other things that have been happening. Ringing bells, chiming clocks. All that rustling and scratching. Mice! Why didn't I think of it before?

Grandad felt very pleased with himself. And he was just thinking, What an old fool I've been – when the bee bride stung him.

'Ow!' yelled Grandad, dropping her on to the floor. He'd heard that bees could sometimes sting after they were dead, but surely not a hundred years after?

He hopped about, flapping his stinging hand. He couldn't blame mice this time. Or his imagination. For there, clear as day on his palm, was a red pinprick.

He looked down. Oh no! When he'd stamped his feet in pain he'd crushed the tiny bee bride.

He knelt down on creaky knees to have a look. Could she be repaired? But there was nothing left to repair. Just a yellow smear and some threads of silk ground into the floorboards.

Grandad wasn't easily rattled. He'd been a rear

gunner in Bomber Command in World War II. He had had lots of close shaves.

But that didn't prepare him for what was happening now in Nursery Rhyme Land.

He felt his old heart race like stampeding cattle. The candles flickered creepily in the draught. What next?

That's when Liam came in.

As soon as Liam saw Grandad he thought, What's wrong? Grandad looked wild-eyed, half crazy, as if he was completely losing his marbles.

Then Grandad saw Jessica. 'What are you doing here?' he said sternly. 'You made a right fool out of me, young lady.'

'I'm sorry, Mr Clamp,' said Jessica. 'I really am. But I've brought your trousers back.'

'My trousers!' cried Grandad, as if he was greeting an old friend. Before Liam could stop him he'd rushed in the back room to put them on.

This is going to be difficult, thought Liam. He knew it would be. How was he going to tell Grandad that his precious trousers must be destroyed?

Then, to his surprise, Jessica said exactly what he was wondering.

'Can't we let your grandad keep the trousers? It wouldn't do any harm. They don't work without Rabbit's teeth, do they?'

'I don't think so,' said Liam. There seemed to be some peculiar kind of chemistry between the teeth and the trousers that brought Rabbit back.

But then Jessica spoke the other thoughts that were in his head. From being on opposite sides, they were suddenly working as a team. Even reading each other's minds.

'It's risky though, isn't it?' said Jessica. She shuddered. She was thinking of Gran with Rabbit's voice coming out of her mouth, Rabbit's expression on her face. Rabbit *seemed* a cringing, whining character, thought Jessica. But he was very powerful. He could control the bodies and brains of toothless wrinklies as if they were robots.

'No!' she said to Liam, her voice suddenly decisive. 'There are too many things we don't know. It's too dangerous. What if Rabbit *can* come back with just the trousers? What if he finds a way? What if he comes back at other times, not just on your Grandpa Clamp's anniversary?'

'Nightmare,' agreed Liam.

Once a year he might just about cope with. But every day? Every day listening to details of Rabbit's dog-dung collecting days? And how was he going to tell Mum, when Grandad turned into Rabbit?

Nightmare again, thought Liam. Mum had a scientific brain. She needed explanations. And there are some things that just can't be explained.

'OK,' agreed Liam. 'We've got to be cruel to be kind. Those trousers will have to go.'

He didn't want to leave the slightest gap, the slightest chance, that would let Rabbit come back from the past. Or Rabbit would be in there, as Grandad would say, like a rat up a drainpipe.

Grandad came parading in wearing his favourite trousers. They seemed to be the one thing he could trust in a world that was out to get him. He licked his poor, stinging palm. Even Nursery Rhyme Land was turning against him now.

'Hot ding! I'm really glad to have these back!' he said, beaming a forgiving smile at Jessica.

Liam cleared his throat. He struggled to find the right words. 'Look, Grandad, I've got something to tell you. It's bad news.'

Outside Nursery Rhyme Land, Mrs Porteous was lurking, spying through a hole in a wooden shutter. She couldn't make anything out. It was a jumble of shadows and candle glow.

Clink, clink, went the silver spurs on her snake-skin boots. She should have silenced them with cotton wool. They would give her away.

'Rubbish!' Grandad was yelling. 'Haunted trousers? Talking teeth? What a load of old codswallop!'

He just wouldn't listen; he was getting really worked up. He couldn't cope with more bad news. His brain was overloaded already. 'I mean, I know I've been too trusting in some things.' He threw a meaningful glance at Jessica. 'But I'm not completely round the bend!'

Liam thought, I'm not doing very well here.

He even got Rabbit's teeth out of his pocket.

He was careful to keep them out of Grandad's reach. He just wanted to *show* them to him – 'I'm not kidding you, Grandad. These teeth have sinister power!' – in a desperate attempt to make his argument more convincing. Nether of them noticed what was going on in the background.

Mayhem was breaking out in Nursery Rhyme Land, as if the animals suddenly realized that time was running out. That Grandpa Clamp's hundredth anniversary was almost over. And there might never be another one.

It started slowly, with a scuffling, a sort of dry rustling, a scratching of shrivelled claws. The weasel's bell tinkled, the Hickory Dickory Dock clock chimed ever so softly, as if it was giving a signal. Grandad probably wouldn't have noticed it anyway, even if he hadn't been shouting at Liam. He'd got used to strange noises on Grandpa Clamp's anniversaries.

But he would probably have noticed the next thing. Like someone punching out a broken car windscreen, a hole appeared in the shattered glass of The Three Little Kittens case. Two eyes peered out. They were blue eyes. They belonged to the white kitten who'd lost her mittens (and her ears).

Some more broken glass tinkled on to the table. The hole got bigger. The candle flames flickered wildly. The shadows on the walls did a frenzied dance. The whole place was whispering, moving, creaking …

Jessica turned round. 'Look!' she screamed, pointing a trembling finger.

As Liam turned, startled, the teeth he'd been clasping so tightly sprang out of his grip. Grandad caught them in mid air and stuffed them greedily into his gob. His face sagged, his body cringed.

'And they only give me a farthing a sack. *Clack*,' a voice whined, 'no matter 'ow full up it was!'

Rabbit was back.

Suddenly, the glass in all the display cases splintered. *Crack, crack, crack, crack,* like gunshot. Animals, birds and insects began tumbling out. The Nursery Rhyme creatures were free at last. And they only had one goal – revenge.

They really wanted to get Grandpa Clamp. But

Grandpa Clamp had declined to come back through time to face his victims. So his apprentice would have to do.

Liam was too stunned to speak or move. He could only watch as the half-rotten army homed in on Grandad. They were still pouring out of their cases: kittens, birds, weasels, mice. In the eerie yellow candle glow they shuffled, fluttered, limped across the floor.

Squeak, squeak. That was the weasel's bike. It needed oiling. Constable Weasel was leading the grisly crew. His razor teeth glittered. The kittens were close behind, their claws already out. Their silly, frilly frocks fell off in rags as they moved. Lots of other bits fell off the animals. As they dragged themselves towards Grandad, they left a trail of wings, beaks, claws. But somehow they still kept going.

Right at the back was the Hickory Dickory Dock mouse. By now, he was hopping along on only three legs. One of his front paws – and his tail – had just fallen off. But, like Terminator, he would never, ever give up.

'Run, Grandad!' The warning exploded from Liam's mouth. But he'd forgotten that Grandad wasn't there.

'Oi!' protested Rabbit, alarmed. 'What's all this, then?'

He was crouched, huddled up in a corner. It wasn't Rabbit Liam was bothered about. They couldn't hurt him; he was dead already. It was poor Grandad's *living* body that was going to suffer the damage.

Outside, Mrs Porteous was rubbing her eyes. The animals of Nursery Rhyme Land, turning against their owner? But she didn't stop to think, *You're seeing things.* Jessica was in there. She was in danger! Mrs Porteous galloped round to the front of the building. She intended to charge in there like the cavalry.

'Gerrof wiv you!'

A blackbird from Sing a Song of Sixpence reached Rabbit first. Its dusty wing slapped him across the head.

'Ow!' yelled Rabbit, rubbing Grandad's smarting skull.

Rabbit swiped at the bird. It broke apart like dry sticks. Fell to the ground in a cloud of sawdust. The other blackbirds attacked him. Their giant shadows flapped on the walls. Soon, you couldn't see Rabbit for birds. In a black cloud they hopped and fluttered round him, trying to peck him. Rabbit, remembering his crow-scaring days, waved Grandad's arms like windmills.

'Shoo! Shoo! Git away, yer ugly brutes!'

Some disintegrated into heaps of feathers.

But it was the kittens he needed to fear. The Hickory Dickory Dock mouse was still limping across the floor. But many of the other animals had had to give up because, like the blackbird, they'd fallen to bits. Those ancient decaying bodies just couldn't stand the strain.

But the kittens crawled on, following the weasel's squeaky bike. If Grandpa Clamp wasn't there, then Rabbit was better than nothing. He was a villain too. Not as bad as Grandpa. But he had stuffed them into that sack –

The door to Nursery Rhyme Land burst open.

A huge Stetson hat filled the frame.

'Gran!' yelled Jessica. 'You've got to save Mr Clamp.'

Even in this crisis, her brain was still working. She didn't try to explain about Rabbit. It would only waste precious time.

Mrs Porteous's amazed eyes took in the scene. Like Grandad, she was not easily rattled. She'd seen lots of strange things in her life. But when she saw Mr Clamp being mobbed by his own stuffed animals, even she was lost for words.

She opened her mouth. Brilliant-white, modern, false gnashers gleamed. 'What –?' she began.

'Just don't ask!' yelled Jessica.

Liam said, 'Quick! Get the Hummer!'

He waded through the decrepit, rag-bag army. The bridegroom fly scrunched underfoot. He didn't even see it.

He whispered urgently in Mrs Porteous's ear. She nodded. And with one stunned look backwards, she disappeared.

Constable Weasel had stopped peddling. He

couldn't get off his bike – his feet were glued to the pedals. He just sat there, his snaky body stooped over the handlebars, waiting for the kittens to catch up.

'It weren't my fault!' a voice wailed out of Grandad's mouth. 'I was only doing what Master said!'

The Three Kittens had finally reached Rabbit. They were minus various bits of body. The earless white cat had lost its tail on the way. But they still had a few needle-sharp teeth left. And between them, they had several claws. The other animals, those that were still in one piece, stopped moving. There was a deadly silence in Nursery Rhyme Land. As if in anticipation. They had been waiting over one hundred years to get their own back.

The Hummer came roaring up to Nursery Rhyme Land, its banks of headlights, spotlights, fog lights on full power.

Good old Mrs Porteous! thought Liam.

He was just about to dash over and open the shutters, when she smashed through the front wall.

'Whoops,' said Mrs Porteous, wrestling with the wheel.

She hadn't meant to do that. She had meant to get in as close as possible and shine her lights through the windows, like Liam said. But those darn snake-skin boots had slipped off the brake. And that front wall was flimsy as toilet paper. It did the job nicely though – the inside of the shack was lit up like an airport runway.

Liam and Jessica shielded their eyes from the blinding light, so they didn't see what happened next.

The Hickory Dickory Dock mouse had finally reached Rabbit. Just before the headlights hit, it slipped up his trouser leg and disappeared into the dark.

The other animals weren't so lucky. There was nowhere to hide from the dazzling glare. It was the first time in over a century that they'd been in strong light. Their fragile bodies couldn't stand it. Like Egyptian mummies exposed to daylight, they crumbled to dust where they stood. Nothing was left of The Three Little Kittens but three tiny pairs of Victorian button-up boots that stood empty, in a pitiful row on the floor. And three pairs of glass eyes, which rolled like marbles under a table.

The bike tipped over with a tiny clink, into the heap of dust that had once been the weasel. His policeman's uniform was dust too. Only his tiny helmet survived.

'Oi!' yelled Rabbit, leaping up. 'There's somefing in me trousers! It's crawling up me leg!'

He danced wildly around, shaking Grandad's poor old body like a rag doll. You could hear Grandad's joints creaking, hear Rabbit's teeth rattling round in his mouth.

In a panic, Rabbit ripped at the trousers, trying to stop the horrid scrabbling and scratching inside. The ancient seams pinged apart. Thread unravelled. Soon the cat-skin trousers hung in tatters.

Rabbit shrieked a final frantic, 'Stop it! Stop it! It's nipping me, *clack*! Then the teeth shot out his mouth. Instantly, he went back into history, where it was safe.

His teeth, of course, stayed in the present. Driven by strong springs, they bounced twice, did a great kangaroo leap out of the door, right under the wheels of Mrs Porteous's Hummer.

The Hickory Dickory Dock mouse was hanging on desperately to Grandad's baggy Y-fronts. Then its other front paw fell off. It tumbled back down his trouser leg. Once it hit bright light it dissolved, like the other Nursery Rhyme animals, into a sad little pile of dust.

Mrs Porteous snapped off her lights. Suddenly Nursery Rhyme Land seemed pitch black. There wasn't even candle glow. They had blown out in the breeze that came through the Hummer-shaped hole in the shack.

Nothing moved. Then Mrs Porteous reversed her jeep slowly out of Nursery Rhyme Land, back on to the road. Something crunched under her big front tyres. She didn't notice.

Liam's eyes felt dazzled. He could still see white flashing lights. He blinked, once, twice, to try and get used to the gloom.

He finally opened his eyes – to a scene of

devastation. Smashed glass, scraps of costume, and heaps and heaps of grey dust that was blowing away through a great gap in the wall. You could see the sea across the road. Its waves were silver in the moonlight.

'Sorry, Grandad, sorry!' said Liam, his hands flying to his mouth in horror. 'We had to do it.'

In his distress, he'd forgotten it was a waste of time talking to Grandad. Because Rabbit was still inside Grandad's body.

But then Grandad's weak, shaky voice said, 'What's going on?'

Liam cried, 'Grandad, it's you!'

His first thought wasn't, Where are Rabbit's teeth? He didn't think about them until later.

Then Jessica said, 'Mr Clamp, I'm sorry about your trousers. I'm sorry about Nursery Rhyme Land.'

'Eh?' said Grandad gazing down at his trousers. They looked as if they'd been in a shredder. 'Eh?' he said again, staring, in a dazed way, at the chaos around him and the splintered hole where the wall had once been.

'We had to,' repeated Liam gently. 'I'm sorry, Grandad.'

Brringg!

Grandad jumped a mile. But it wasn't the weasel's bike. It was the alarm on his wrist watch.

He'd forgotten he'd set it for midnight. Grandpa Clamp's hundredth anniversary was well and truly over.

Chapter Nine

Mrs Porteous was parking her Hummer back at the bungalow. There was a double yellow line on the sea front. She was a responsible citizen, president of APUP. She didn't want to get a parking ticket.

Meanwhile, back at the wreckage of Nursery Rhyme Land, Grandad had gone into the back room to change into his grey slacks. He threw the cat-skin trousers in the bin. That was all they were fit for now.

Liam looked at Jessica. 'He took it quite well, didn't he?' he said, amazed. 'Except, do you think you should have blamed your gran?'

Jessica shrugged. 'They hate each other anyway,' she said. 'He'll just hate her a bit more now.'

Liam had been struggling. He'd tried to explain again about Rabbit. But he could see from Grandad's angry expression that he didn't want to listen to *that* story.

Then Jessica saved his life. She'd used her reporter's skills – she'd been really convincing. And it had been the truth, well, more or less. She'd told Grandad that Mrs Porteous had lost control of the jeep and crashed, with headlights blazing, into Nursery Rhyme Land. And, 'Everything just got thrown all over the place,' and Grandad had been briefly knocked out by a flying blackbird.

Grandad said three things. 'I thought my head hurt.' Then he said, 'Women drivers!' Then he said, 'Pity she didn't finish the job. Save the bulldozers the trouble.'

He didn't believe Jessica's story. He wasn't a fool. He knew there had to be much more to what had happened than that. But it didn't really matter now. He didn't even want to think about it. Because, whatever had happened, it all amounted to the same thing. He was free at last of Nursery

Rhyme Land. It had turned out, in these last few years, to be a millstone round his neck.

He was sorry for Liam though. Liam had been the only reason he'd kept the place going.

Poor lad, he was thinking as he changed his trousers in the back room. He won't be taking over Nursery Rhyme Land after all. I bet he's really upset.

'You're not going to write about any of this, are you?' Liam asked Jessica. He was recovering fast from the destruction of Nursery Rhyme Land. Strangely, he was in quite a happy and carefree mood. He felt a bit guilty about that.

Jessica didn't answer. So Liam asked her again. 'You're not going to, are you?'

Still Jessica hesitated. It was very tempting. It would make a great story, and make her dad really take notice of her. She could see the headline now: *NIGHTMARE IN NURSERY RHYME LAND.*

But in the end she sighed and said, 'No, I don't want to cause any more trouble for Mr Clamp.

And no one would believe me anyway.'

Clink, clink.

What was that sound? It was the jingle of spurs on rattlesnake-skin boots. Mrs Porteous came striding through the hole in the wall where the door had once been.

'Is everyone safe?' she asked. Eagle-eyed, she checked the room. Even she was surprised. Nursery Rhyme Land didn't exist any more. The stuffed animals were dust. Even the dust was blowing out to sea.

'Now, can someone please tell me what's been going on?' she demanded. 'Because I think I'm going round the bend.'

'Well, Gran, it's like this,' said Jessica, taking a deep breath, as if she was going to be talking for ages.

Mrs Porteous preferred action to long explanations. Impatiently, she waved Jessica to be quiet.

'Don't bother,' she said. 'I don't think I want to know. I'm just really glad to see the back of this place at long last!'

'So am I,' said Grandad, coming out of the back room looking dapper in his grey slacks with his own false teeth in his mouth.

Eh? thought Liam. He opened his mouth to exclaim, 'I thought you'd be really sad!' But he didn't get the chance because Grandad had seen Mrs Porteous's outfit.

'I didn't know you were a Wild West fan,' he said.

The president of APUP looked suspicious. She didn't know Grandad still carried a torch for her. She couldn't recall their childhood romance. She just thought he was a nasty old man.

But then Jessica chipped in. 'Grandma,' she said, 'Mr Clamp is OK. Really he is.' Then she moved closer and whispered a warning. 'Anyway, I saw you trying on his cat-skin trousers. So I'd be nice to him if I were you.'

Liam, who'd only heard the first bit, felt really proud of Jessica. Sticking up for Grandad made up for the other things she'd done. Except for writing the fainting goat story of course. Mum and Milton were still in terrible trouble about that.

Their jobs were on the line.

'Hot ding!' said Grandad excitedly. 'You sure as shootin' look mighty fine there, ma'am!'

Oh no! thought Liam, squirming with shame, he's talking that cheesy cowboy talk!

'Shouldn't that be hot *dang*?' Mrs Porteous corrected him sternly. She was a stickler for authenticity.

Grandad was crestfallen. He'd been saying hot ding for years. And now he'd discovered it should be hot dang! He felt like an utter fool!

Mrs Porteous saw his embarrassment. She also saw Jessica frowning, and remembered her whispered warning. So she said, with a pleasant smile, 'Never mind. What does it matter? What's a ding or a dang between Wild West fans?'

'Do you want to see General Custer's false teeth?' asked Grandad, encouraged. He looked round in a vague sort of way. 'I had them just now. Where have they got to?'

Suddenly, Liam wondered that too.

'Never mind,' said Grandad. 'I've got some frying-pan arrows through the back.' He cast his

eye over Mrs Porteous's boots. 'Pardon me, ma'am, but ain't those genuine rattlesnake-skin boots you're wearing?'

'You're darned tootin',' Mrs Porteous found herself replying.

She was beginning to think that Jessica was right. Perhaps she'd been too hasty in judging Mr Clamp. Anyone who could recognize *genuine* rattlesnake-skin boots couldn't be all bad.

Grandad and Mrs Porteous disappeared into the back room. Liam looked at Jessica. 'Did you see where Rabbit's false teeth went? We can't take any chances. They must be destroyed.'

They searched through the wreckage of Nursery Rhyme Land. Liam rescued some things from the shattered glass cases – the tiny silver tea set, the bee bride's withered bouquet. He picked up the weasel's bike and put all the sad relics of Nursery Rhyme Land in a heap on a table.

Mrs Porteous came jingling in with Grandad. To Liam's amazement, they seemed on quite friendly terms. Mrs Porteous inspected the things on the table. 'I think you're in luck here,' she told

Grandad. 'You might earn yourself some cash.'

'I always thought that silver tea set might be worth a bob or two,' said Grandad. 'It's an exact copy, in miniature of course, of one that George III was given at his coronation.'

'No, not that!' said Mrs Porteous. 'That's made out of tin, it's not worth 2p! It's that weasel's bike I'm on about. Friends of the Weasel would pay a small fortune for that.'

'Hum,' said Grandad thoughtfully, blowing the dust off the bike. 'That's certainly worth knowing.' He stashed it away in his coat pocket.

After Jessica and Mrs Porteous had gone home, Liam was suddenly hit by a terrible weariness. He knew that finding Rabbit's teeth was a top priority. But he just couldn't keep his eyes open.

'Come on, son,' said Grandad. 'It's way past your bedtime. Let's go back to the flat.' He took one last look round Nursery Rhyme Land, at the great gaping hole in the wall. 'Well, at least I don't have to lock up tonight,' he said to Liam. 'There's nothing left to steal.'

'Grandad,' said Liam, yawning, 'what did you

mean just now when you said you were glad to see the back of Nursery Rhyme Land?'

Grandad was tired too. Too tired to pretend any more.

'I'm sorry, son, but this place was getting to be a real headache. I just didn't want the responsibility any longer. I told Mrs Porteous in the back room. I said, "To tell the truth, I'm grateful to you!"'

'But that's just what I feel as well!' interrupted Liam. 'I never wanted to take over Nursery Rhyme Land. I'm glad to see the back of it too.'

'Well, well,' said Grandad, shaking his head. 'Hot ding! I mean, hot dang! Who'd have thought it? You learn something new every day. Mind you, your Grandpa Clamp would turn in his grave if he heard us talking like this.'

'Who cares about him?' said Liam. 'You always said all the animals in Nursery Rhyme Land died of natural causes – of old age or because they got sick or something. But they didn't *all*. He killed some of them, didn't he? Why didn't you tell me about that?'

'I didn't want to upset you,' said Grandad, looking a bit embarrassed.

'But my own Great Great Great Grandpa was a cat killer!'

'I wouldn't be surprised,' said Grandad. 'But times were different then. You mustn't be too harsh on him.'

Why not? thought Liam.

But he could see there was no point in going on about it. Where Grandpa Clamp was concerned, he and Grandad would never agree.

But talking about Grandpa Clamp reminded Liam of something else. Another question he had to ask. 'Grandad,' he said, 'what happened to Rabbit, Grandpa's Clamp's apprentice?'

'It's a bit hazy,' said Grandad. 'It's just old family stories. But they say he got very ill. He died of pneumonia when he was only fourteen. I told you, he had a tragic life.'

As they walked to the door, Liam hung his head and shuffled his feet through the splintered glass. He wished he'd never asked Grandad now.

Knowing how Rabbit died made him feel really sad.

He kept hearing Rabbit's voice in his head, the awful details of his miserable life. 'Me knees and elbows is always scabbed. I gets beat black and blue. Me hands, they look like skellington's bones.' Liam wished he'd listened more carefully.

I should have taped his story, thought Liam. Or written it down or something. Now it's lost for ever.

Together, Grandad and Liam walked out of Nursery Rhyme Land.

'Wait a sec,' said Grandad. 'There's a few things I should keep. Like those frying-pan arrows. Mrs Porteous was very interested in those. Wish I could find General Custer's false teeth though. That would really impress her.' He dashed back into the shack.

Liam felt something gritty under his shoes. He looked down. What was that? He saw two crushed metal springs and some yellow bits.

Rabbit's teeth! he thought. They were totally destroyed. Which was just what he wanted, wasn't it? But then, in the gutter, he saw something glint under the street light. It was a human tooth, one of Rabbit's; somehow it had escaped being flattened by Mrs Porteous's Hummer.

Liam knew he should have left it there. To be pecked at by seagulls, covered with litter, or kicked down a drain. But a voice in his head begged, 'Don't leave me here in the gutter!' So he bent down, picked up the tooth and put it into his trouser pocket.

Chapter Ten

The next morning, Grandad and Liam were woken up by the sound of a growling engine. Grandad poked his head out the flat window and tried to focus his bleary eyes. Mrs Porteous and Jessica were there, in the Hummer.

'Come on,' yelled Mrs Porteous. 'We've got to go to the university. Hasn't Liam told you?'

'Told me what?' said Grandad.

'About all the trouble – the fainting goat. Don't you read the newspapers?'

'I've given up reading the newspapers,' said Grandad.

'But isn't Dr Janet Cooper Liam's mum? Jessica says she is.'

Liam walked, yawning, into Grandad's bedroom.

'What's this you should have told me, son, about the trouble at the university? Is your mum involved?'

Liam looked embarrassed. He nodded.

'Mum and Milton cloned a goat. And it went wrong. And Jessica wrote a story about it. Now everyone knows and Mum might lose her job.'

'Why didn't you tell me?'

'I thought you had enough problems of your own,' said Liam, 'without hearing about anyone else's.'

What, even my own daughter's? thought Grandad. But he didn't say it. It wasn't Liam's fault that his grandad and mum were like strangers. Grandad sighed and poked his head back out the window.

'I'm a bit in the dark about all this,' he confessed to Mrs Porteous. 'I've had a lot on my mind lately.'

'Never mind!' Mrs Porteous yelled back briskly. 'Just get dressed. I'll explain on the way.'

They sped back down the sea front, with the wind whipping back their hair, past Mrs

Porteous's bungalow and Nursery Rhyme Land.

A yellow JCB was already there, moving in to make the shack into matchwood. Grandad tried not to look. He was relieved to be free. But he couldn't help feeling a pang of regret.

You've got to make a fresh start! he scolded himself.

But fresh starts can be scary. Especially when you've been living in Nursery Rhyme Land for fifty years.

Then Mrs Porteous took his mind off Nursery Rhyme Land.

She slowed down to a sedate thirty miles per hour. 'John Tinsley!' she yelled at Grandad.

'The ultimate showman!' Grandad yelled back.

'I should have thought of it sooner!' replied Mrs Porteous.

'What are they talking about?' said Liam to Jessica. Jessica had been very quiet since he'd got in the Hummer, which wasn't like her at all. She seemed to be nervous about something. Which wasn't like her either.

'That fainting goat,' said Jessica. 'There's more to it than I thought. I think your mum's going to be really mad with me!'

Liam opened his mouth: 'Why?'

But just then Mrs Porteous hit the accelerator, and the wind-rush and engine-roar drowned out his question.

At the university, Milton came staggering back into the building. His hair was wilder than ever. He was puffed out. His high-top trainers felt sizzling hot.

'Haven't those kids got anything better to do?' he gasped.

This was the tenth time that morning he'd caught them creeping through bushes, ready to leap out and shout 'Boo!' The tenth time he'd chased them off, giggling like loonies. Those kids sure could run!

Scaring Snowdrop was the latest 'dare'. Word must have spread. Little kids for miles around were trying to sneak into the university. Along with the TV crews and newspaper reporters.

Liam's mum watched anxiously from her office window. She was worried to death and bone-weary. She and Milton had been here all night, keeping Snowdrop safe. At least Snowdrop didn't seem worried. She didn't have a clue about all the commotion she'd caused. She had no idea she was a freak. She was happily frisking about in her pen, eating grass.

But, for the hundredth time, Liam's mum thought, She can't stay here; she'll never get any peace.

'Why don't they just clear off?' she murmured, looking at the TV vans and cars outside the fence. But she knew they wouldn't clear off. Not while there was a sensational story to tell.

Oh no, thought Milton. Here we go again.

He'd seen some more people tip-toeing round the corner of the building. He opened the EXIT doors gently and got ready to rush out.

'Liam!' he cried. He clapped his hand over his mouth. Too late.

Whump. Snowdrop dropped in a dead faint, her four little legs sticking up stiff as broom handles.

One, two, three, four …

Grandad and Mrs Porteous didn't turn a hair.

'Where's this goat from, young man?' Mrs Porteous asked Milton, as Snowdrop scrambled to her feet and came over to nuzzle Mrs Porteous's hand.

'Tennessee,' said Milton. 'That's where the cell we cloned her from was taken. From our colleagues in Tennessee, USA.'

'Hot ding! I mean, dang!' Grandad gave a great cowboy whoop. He couldn't help himself.

Whump.

'Sorry,' said Grandad, looking sheepish.

As Snowdrop twitched herself awake, Mrs Porteous whispered, 'I was right.' She wasn't at all surprised. She was usually right all the time.

Liam was beginning to think that she and Grandad were as mad as each other. Perhaps being taken over by Rabbit had scrambled their brains.

'Wait a minute,' said Milton, frowning at Jessica. 'Isn't this the kid who spilled the beans about Snowdrop?'

'It's all right, Milton,' said Liam.
'She's with me. And she's not looking
for bad news this time.'

'No,' said Jessica, suddenly breaking her
silence. 'We've come with some good news.'

'About time,' said Milton wearily. Even he was
looking harassed. The spring had quite gone out
of his step. Liam thought, Poor Mum. I was too
wrapped up in Nursery Rhyme Land. I should've
been more help.

The same thoughts were in Grandad's mind.
But he wasn't depressed. He seemed amazingly
bright and chirpy.

'Take me to my daughter, son!' he ordered
Milton. 'I think she's going to be very pleased to
see me.'

'She's with me,' said Liam before Mum could
object to Jessica. But Mum was so surprised to see
Grandad that she didn't notice Jessica at all.

'Dad!' she said. 'What are you doing here?'

'Actually,' said Grandad, 'we've come to tell you
a story.'

'I don't mean to be rude,' said Liam's mum, as the phone rang on and on in the background. 'But I haven't got time for stories.'

'Just two minutes,' said Grandad, taking the phone off the hook. 'I'll let Mrs Porteous do the honours.'

Mum looked confused. She raised her eyebrows at Liam, as if to say, 'What's going on here?' Hadn't he told her that Mrs Porteous and Grandad were deadly enemies?

But Liam was no help. All he did was shrug and raise his eyebrows.

'No, you do the honours,' insisted Mrs Porteous politely to Grandad.

'No, *you*,' said Grandad. 'You discovered it first.'

'For heaven's sake!' said Jessica. '*Somebody* tell her! Back in Tennessee around 1880 there was this guy called John Tinsley –'

'The ultimate showman,' interrupted Grandad.

'The ultimate conman, more like,' corrected Mrs Porteous.

'You tell it then!' said Jessica.

'Right,' said Grandad, who didn't need asking twice. 'Well, this John Tinsley bloke made his living travelling around Tennessee selling medicines. And he claimed to have this wonderful tonic that he said could cure *any* animal – cows, horses, goats.'

Liam didn't have a clue where this was leading. But perhaps Mum did. She seemed suddenly very interested.

'The point is,' said Mrs Porteous, muscling in, 'he had four goats that he used in his demonstrations.'

'And he'd bring them on,' said Grandad, taking over, 'and tell these simple farming folk, "Watch this, folks, this goat has got a real bad case of palsy. But I'm aiming to heal her right up, in front of your very eyes!" Then he'd clap or something, make a loud noise and *whump* the goat would faint –'

'I get you!' said Mum eagerly. 'Then he'd dose the goat with his tonic and after ten seconds she'd get up and people would think it was some kind of miracle cure.'

'Exactly!' said Grandad. 'And then he'd high-tail it out of there before folks found out his miracle cure was a fake.'

'So what happened to his goats then?' asked Mum.

'Ah,' said Grandad. 'Now that's where it gets interesting. Maybe Tennessee got too hot for him. Too many farmers chasing him for their money back! Anyway, he left in a hurry. But *before* he left,' said Grandad significantly, 'he sold his fainting goats to a farmer called Mayberry –'

'Who bred them!' Mum finished the sentence as if she and Grandad were a double act.

'Exactly!' said Grandad and Mrs Porteous together.

Liam was looking at Mum then at Grandad and back again. He was obviously missing something. Why was he still in the dark while everyone else, including Milton, had faces that were bright with understanding?

'So what happened to John Tinsley?' asked Liam. It was obviously the wrong question.

'He doesn't matter,' said Mrs Porteous impatiently. 'No one ever heard of him again. It's the *goats* that are important. The point is, Tennessee fainting goats still exist. They're a rare breed. Hardly anyone knows about them. But some people still keep them over in America.'

'What for?' asked Liam. 'Whole herds of goats that go *zonk* every time a car backfires! Who wants them?' Again it seemed to be the wrong question.

'*I* do, for a start!' declared Mrs Porteous. 'They're such sweet little things. They need special tender loving care. From someone who understands animals. I wouldn't mind breeding them myself. It would be a real challenge.'

'You're darn tootin',' agreed Grandad, who happened to be looking for a new challenge himself. One that involved *live* animals would be a real novelty.

It was Mum who finally explained it all to Liam. 'Don't you see, Liam? What Grandad's just told me is brilliant news. It means that Snowdrop isn't our fault. She's not some one-off laboratory freak. There's are lots of others like her back in America.'

'Yeah,' added Milton. 'She's entirely normal. For a Tennessee fainting goat, that is. She's just doing what fainting goats do.'

'We must have got sent one by mistake,' said Mum. 'Some kind of mix-up with goat cells back in the States.'

'So the university is off the hook.' Jessica summed it up.

'No thanks to you, kid,' said Milton.

But, to Liam's surprise, Mum chipped in. 'She's not to blame,' said Mum. 'We should have known. But I'd never heard of Tennessee fainting goats. Not until Dad told us.'

She smiled gratefully at Grandad. And Grandad smiled back. 'Happy to help,' he said.

'I'm sorry about Nursery Rhyme Land,' said Liam's mum. 'All your hard work. You really looked after that place.'

Grandad shrugged. 'I'll get over it. In fact,' he said, 'that reminds me. Nursery Rhyme Land might have done me a big favour.' He got the weasel's bike out of his pocket. 'Are you on the Internet?'

'Help yourself,' said Mum, pointing to the computer on her desk.

'You'll have to show me,' said Grandad.

'Wait a sec,' said Mum. 'I'd better deal with that lot out there first. Tell them the truth about fainting goats. Then perhaps they'll leave Snowdrop alone.'

'You leave that to me,' said Mrs Porteous, who'd already appointed herself Snowdrop's protector. 'I'll deal with them. I'm good at that kind of thing. Come on,' she said, crooking a finger at Milton. 'I need you. You're a boffin, aren't you? You can blind them with science.' And she went striding out to the waiting TV vans, with Milton trotting like an obedient puppy behind her.

While Mum and Grandad tapped at the keys, Liam and Jessica whispered to each other. After all, they shared secrets between them. Secrets that none of the grown-ups knew.

'Did you find Rabbit's teeth?' asked Jessica.

She was more talkative now. She'd expected a very unfriendly reception at the university. She'd expected to take all the blame. It was a big relief that Liam's mum didn't think it was that simple.

'Yes, I found them,' said Liam. 'Your gran's Hummer crushed them to bits.'

'And the trousers are all ripped up.'

'Yep, Grandad chucked them out.'

He wondered whether to tell her about the tooth that survived. The one that was still in the pocket of his combats. But when Jessica said happily: 'That's that then. That creepy Rabbit can't ever come back!' he decided not to.

And anyway, just then Grandad gave a delighted shout. 'There it is! We've found it! That's the Friends of the Weasel web site.'

Liam and Jessica rushed to look over his shoulder. There it was, with a pin-up of a wily-looking weasel. And its Weasel Thought of the Week: *Never Disturb a Sleeping Weasel*.

Underneath it were lots of amazing weasel facts.

'Who'd have thought it,' said Grandad, putting on his specs and reading one. 'Did you know that folk used to think that there was a *smaller* species of weasel, called a *Finger* Weasel? And did you know that –'

'So, what do you want to do?' interrupted Mum, before he read out any more.

Grandad glanced at the weasel bike on Mum's desk. 'I want to put an advert on this web site,' he said. 'I've got it here.'

He took a crumpled piece of paper out of his pocket. He'd already written it out.

'A unique chance for weasel lovers,' it read. *'For sale: Very rare weasel memorabilia. Genuine antique weasel bike. One hundred and fifty years old! As used by Constable Weasel in Who Killed Cock Robin? Any offers?'*

Chapter Eleven

Months had passed since the creatures of
Nursery Rhyme Land had dissolved into
dust. There was an ice-cream stall now where
Grandad's shack had been.

Liam still carried Rabbit's tooth around. He
didn't know why he was keeping it or what he was
keeping it for. He just couldn't seem to throw it
away.

'It's our stop,' said Liam to Jessica.

They clambered down the stairs of the bus.
They were miles out of town, deep in the
countryside. They were going to do what they did
every Saturday: visit their grandparents.

Jessica and Liam had become best mates.
Liam's other mates couldn't understand it. They

said, 'How did those two get so friendly?'

Apart from the custard survey, they'd never seen Liam even *talking* to Jessica. But they didn't know about the bond between them, about all that had happened on Grandpa Clamp's anniversary.

The bus pulled away. Just along the road, a large notice said, 'FAINTING GOAT FARM. OPEN TO THE PUBLIC.'

There had been lots of things happening in Grandad's life. And in Mrs Porteous's too. They were partners now, in a new enterprise. They bred Tennessee fainting goats. Mum had given them Snowdrop to start off and they had flown in more fainting goats from America. Now there were fields full of them.

'Grandma's put some more notices up,' said Jessica. 'She's going a bit over the top, don't you think?'

'SILENCE!' roared a notice, as they walked up the track to Fainting Goat Farm. 'BE QUIET!' said another. 'NO MOBILES! NO CREAKY

CAGOULS! NO CRYING BABIES!'

Mrs Porteous was fiercely protective of her goats. She had formed a new group, APUG, the Association for the Public Understanding of Goats. She was president of it, of course. And she fired off letters about noisy tractors, crowing cockerels, sheep that *baaed* too loudly. Anything that upset her precious fainting goats. She was having a whale of a time.

Grandad was happy too. It made a wonderful change to be showing kids live creatures instead of stuffed ones.

'Tiny tots *love* visiting Fainting Goat Farm,' he told Liam.

But he was as wrong about that as he'd been about Nursery Rhyme Land. Tiny tots *hated* visiting Fainting Goat Farm because they had to be quiet all the time. Liam never told Grandad the truth, of course. That would have been too cruel.

'Shut up! Shut up!' parents would hiss. They'd be on tenterhooks all the time. Because if tiny tots burst their bubble gum, *pop!* or undid the Velcro fastenings on their coat, *rrrip!* that was that.

Whump. The nearest goat would be belly-up, with its legs in the air. And Mrs Porteous would be on the warpath.

And it was maximum stress for teachers who brought whole classes here, because there'd always be one clever clogs at the back who'd yell, 'Boo!' Several schools had been banned from visiting Fainting Goat Farm.

'Teachers in my day were tough,' sighed Mrs Porteous. 'Teachers these days – they can't control kids at all!'

But with everyone except tiny tots (and parents and teachers) Fainting Goat Farm was a wild success. Fainting goats were trendy pets. Suddenly, everyone wanted one.

The perfect pet for stressed-out people! said Jessica's advert in the Lifestyle section of the Sunday papers. *Lower your blood pressure! Learn how to relax!*

You *had* to relax around fainting goats. You just couldn't be jumpy. No sudden movements. No sudden noise. No hurry or rush.

'I haven't felt so calm in years,' wrote one grateful goat-owner to Grandad. 'And it's all thanks to you, Mr Clamp.'

Grandad framed that letter. He wasn't used to fan mail. For years, all the postman had brought was hate mail to Nursery Rhyme Land.

'And to think that a weasel's bike paid for all this,' Grandad would often marvel, smoking a peaceful pipe and admiring his farmhouse and fields.

The weasel's bike had come up trumps. There had been cut-throat bidding. But in the end, someone had faxed in a late bid from the USA. It was a billionaire who was potty about weasels, who gave bags of cash to weasel charities. He bid a six-figure sum!

Liam and Jessica reached Grandad's house. It had a smart new name plaque outside that said: Home on the Range.

'I think Grandma's moving into Home on the Range,' said Jessica. 'She's put her bungalow up for sale. You don't think they're sweethearts again, do you?'

'Yuk, no,' said Liam, grimacing. He didn't even want to think about it. 'How disgusting! They're too old and wrinkly for that.'

But secretly, Jessica was already making up headlines: *FAINTING GOAT PAIR IN FAIRY-TALE WEDDING*. She daren't imagine any further than that. She kept seeing Gran going down the aisle in a big white Stetson and rattlesnake-skin boots.

Even Gran wouldn't do that, thought Jessica. But she wouldn't have taken a bet on it.

Grandad and Mrs Porteous weren't at the house. They were in the goat pens, next to a big red sign that shrieked 'SHHHHH!'

'Come over here, you two,' whispered Grandad, 'if you want to see a little miracle.'

They tiptoed over.

'Awwwww,' said Liam. A soppy grin spread all over his face.

Snowdrop had had two babies. They were the image of their mum. They were already tottering round on shaky legs.

'Will they faint too?' asked Liam.

As if in answer to his question, they heard a low drone in the distance, like an angry wasp.

It got louder and louder.

'Oh no,' muttered Grandad. 'Low-flying aircraft.'

Suddenly, with an ear-splitting roar, the jet buzzed the farm.

Snowdrop and her babies fainted first. Then *whump, whump, whump, whump.* Fields full of goats went down like skittles. A forest of broomstick legs pointed at the sky.

'I hate it when that happens!' thundered Mrs Porteous. She could yell now the goats were unconscious. She shook her fist at the jet. It was just a dot in the sky.

'I'm sure those pilots do it on purpose. Mark my words, there'll be a letter in the post tomorrow!'

Chapter Twelve

Liam was at the university, hanging around outside the labs. Jessica wasn't with him. This was something he had to do alone. He wasn't even going to tell her about it. It was a secret no one could share.

It was 7 April. Grandpa Clamp's anniversary had rolled round again. Liam thought, I bet I'm the only one who's noticed.

Grandad was too busy with his new life to think much about Nursery Rhyme Land. But, for some reason, Liam remembered. And ever since he had got up that morning, Rabbit's tooth seemed to have been burning a hole in his pocket. And he seemed to hear, inside his head, Rabbit's whiny voice boring him rigid with his biography.

'I nearly got arrested, I did, for stealing me own teef! Did I ever tell you about that?'

Liam was sorry about Rabbit's wretched life, and even more sorry about his tragic, early death. It made him really sad to think about it. But there are only so many details about dog-dung collecting a boy can stand.

'*Great big* dogs were best. I used ter follow 'em round with me shovel.'

This is driving me round the bend, thought Liam.

It was scaring him too, this spooky invasion of his mind. It was almost as if Rabbit was trying to come back again. Liam told himself that was impossible. That Rabbit was stuck for ever in history. He told himself, 'It's just your imagination.'

But he still thought, I've got to get Rabbit out of my head.

Even when he wasn't there, borrowing your grandad's body, you couldn't forget Rabbit. He had a way of clinging to you, of wheedling his way into your life. He pretended to be cringing and humble. But he was much more powerful than he let on.

Suddenly, Liam had a solution. It just came to him, out of the blue. Every time you look at his tooth it reminds you. Give it away. Get rid of it! Then you get rid of Rabbit.

And then, hot on the heels of the first one, came another bright idea. I know who you could give it to!

And that was why he was here now, hanging around the labs, waiting for Milton. He couldn't go in. Children weren't allowed in there.

At last, Milton came bounding out in his white coat.

'Hey, Milton,' said Liam, trying to sound casual, as if he hadn't been waiting for ages. 'I've got something for you.'

'Surprise me!' said Milton.

Liam took Rabbit's tooth out of his pocket. 'It's for your collection of famous teeth,' he told Milton.

'Wow, really?' said Milton. 'Whose is it?'

Liam hesitated. He'd hit a snag – he hadn't

thought this through. Rabbit wasn't famous. Who'd ever heard of Rabbit? He didn't even have a proper name. He was a starving street child, before Great Great Great Grandpa Clamp took him in. His only talents were crow-catching, dog-dung collecting and cat-hunting.

What if Milton wasn't interested? What if he wouldn't take the tooth?

'Er,' Liam lied frantically, 'it's General Custer's. Grandad used to have it on display at Nursery Rhyme Land.'

'You're kidding me!' Milton was really impressed. 'You mean *the* General Custer of Custer's Last Stand? That *is* famous! Is it genuine?'

'Oh yes,' Liam heard himself saying. 'Perfectly genuine.'

'And are you *sure* your grandad doesn't want it?'

'Yes,' said Liam. ' In fact, he'd be really, really grateful if you took it off his hands.'

Milton opened his mouth to ask more questions. But Liam didn't give him the chance. As soon as he'd handed the tooth over, he felt free of the presence of Rabbit. That pestering, creepy voice in his head had vanished. Rabbit was someone else's problem now.

'Bye!' said Liam, making a swift escape on his skateboard.

He gave Mum a cheery wave as he whizzed past her office. Mum came to the door. 'Hey!' she cried. 'You're not allowed to do that in here.' But Liam was long gone.

Milton was tickled pink with his new tooth. It would be the prize of his collection. Even more exciting than Queen Victoria's tooth. He carried it into the lab.

Liam had never asked Milton *why* he collected famous teeth. It had never occurred to him. He didn't really take Milton seriously. He thought he was a little bit crazy.

But people should have taken Milton seriously. Because Milton, in his own weird way, was a scientific genius. He was secretly carrying out experiments after hours. Not even Liam's mum knew about them. It was a good job she didn't. It would have made her hair turn white.

Milton was a long way from his goal. Often, he thought he would never reach it. That it wasn't scientifically possible.

But now, as he held Rabbit's tooth, he felt new inspiration. He could even see where he'd gone wrong. Ideas were sprouting like weeds in his brain.

'*Polymerase … enzymes … DNA sequence,*' Milton began to mutter, as he prepared to drill into what he thought was General Custer's tooth.

Cloning famous people from the past from the DNA inside their teeth suddenly didn't seem like such a wild dream after all.

He felt so confident of success that he even set himself a deadline. He didn't know why he chose this particular date. It just seemed to pop into his head. 'This time next year,' he told himself, 'on this very day, the seventh April, I'll be ready. I shall start to grow a clone of General Custer.'